"I was going to approach the task force years ago when I first heard about it forming," retired officer Young said. "Then got sidetracked with Barbara and everything. So really looking forward to helping in any way that I can. This case has haunted me since I was a rookie on the job."

"Certain cases can do that, can't they?" Bonnie said.

"Seeing those two women with their fingers and thumbs cut off and their faces destroyed is not something I will ever forget."

Bonnie just nodded to that.

"And having the cases go cold and unsolved had to not help," Cavanaugh said.

"Drove me nuts," Young said, laughing lightly to himself. "Barbara wouldn't let me talk about it, I got so obsessed. I even kept some of the evidence when it was going to be discarded twenty years ago. Figured DNA might help if I could get someone to look into it."

Bonnie damn near came out of her chair. "You rescued evidence?"

"I did," Young said, nodding. "Metro evidence department called me one day about twenty years ago and told me that the department was cleaning out old evidence boxes to get more room and asked if I wanted to store some of it. So I got it in the garage. Barbara hated that, let me tell you."

"Clothes?" Cavanaugh asked.

"With bloodstains," Young said, smiling.

"Well, hell," Cavanaugh said, laughing. "Looks like we are in business."

Bonnie could only agree with that. They had just caught their first break.

ALSO BY DEAN WESLEY SMITH

RING GAME

A Cold Poker Gang Mystery

DEAN WESLEY SMITH

wmg
PUBLISHING

Ring Game

Copyright © 2021 by Dean Wesley Smith

All rights reserved

Published by WMG Publishing
Cover and layout copyright © 2021 by WMG Publishing
Cover art copyright © by Vadarshop/Depositphotos
ISBN-13: 978-1-56146-344-2
ISBN-10: 1-56146-344-2

AUTHOR'S NOTE:

RING GAME

Ring Game:

Usually refers to a game being played near a tournament, but not part of the tournament.

PART ONE

The Impossible

PROLOGUE

October 14th, 1980
Outside of Las Vegas, Nevada

Las Vegas Metro Patrol Officer Matthew Young stared at the dead body of the young woman sitting behind the wheel of a new, blue-tinted Chevy. He just flat wanted to be sick. In his first year on the force he had seen some ugly stuff, but this was one of the worst, without a doubt.

Nightmare bad.

The Chevy had been pulled off the two-lane Highway 95 about two miles outside of the city limits of Las Vegas sometime during the night. This road headed northwest toward Reno and didn't see much traffic at all at night.

The body had been posed behind the steering wheel as if she had been driving. Not much chance of that.

Young looked away and out over the desert around him, forcing himself to take deep, long breaths of the crystal-fresh air. Right now the sun was just barely cresting the mountains to the east of Vegas and the air had a sharp bite to it, so he could see his own breath.

There was nothing but open desert and scrub brush around where the car had been parked. Closest building was back a good half mile toward Vegas. Nothing at all in the other direction for miles and miles.

The only reason he had stopped to check on this Chevy was because the lights of the car had been left on and he could tell from the looks of them that the battery was almost dead. He figured the driver was asleep or might need some help.

But the woman behind the wheel hadn't been the driver and was far, far from needing help.

Young turned back to study the scene while he waited for his back-up and the coroner's office to arrive. He didn't dare touch anything, but he might see something that would help.

The woman now sitting peacefully had clearly been dead long before she reached this spot. From the looks of her hair and shape, she was young and had a trim figure. She had on a blue thin sweater over a white blouse and a light-blue matching skirt. Being single and only a year out of the academy, he didn't know enough about clothes to know if they were expensive or not.

There was no purse or identification in the car that he could see, but he knew enough to not do more than look from the outside at the interior of the car.

And without something like that kind of identification, Young doubted this woman would ever be identified. All ten of her fingers had been cut off, the stubs of her hands resting peacefully in her lap. Her mouth and most of her face had been destroyed by a blast from some gun, more than likely a shotgun.

What was strange was that there was almost no blood on her clothes and none that he could see in the car at all.

This was the second body exactly like this he had seen in his first year on the job. The first time he had been called to the scene later to work traffic as they took the woman's body out of the car. He had been sick on that one in the ditch beside the road when he made the mistake of watching them take the poor woman from the car. And the body had been found, also in a Chevy, and also on this same road.

In fact, he wouldn't doubt if it was pretty much in this exact same spot.

The first young woman also had all her fingers gone and her mouth and face totally destroyed. Clearly both had been killed by the same sicko and for some reason the killer did not want his victims to be identified.

So the sicko had killed them somewhere else, destroyed their teeth and mouth and face and then cut off their fingers. No prints, no dental, nothing.

Young had heard of no leads on the first case and unless they got real lucky, this poor girl would end up with no family or friends knowing she was dead.

No one deserved what had happened to her and no one deserved not being identified.

He turned and walked through the cold morning back to his patrol car to wait for the help that was coming. Somehow, even though he was new on the job, he would work to find out who did this, move this case forward as much as he could. Find the animal who did this.

Or go to his grave trying.

CHAPTER ONE

January 24th, 2019
Las Vegas, Nevada

Retired Detective Benson Cavanaugh walked beside his partner, retired Detective Bonnie State out of the older-style suburban home where the Cold Poker Gang task force meeting was being held. In his right hand he held a very thick red file that looked like an official police file except for the big black stamp "Copy" on the cover.

It would be his and Bonnie's second case to work together. And at first glance, the case looked even more impossible than the first one they had just solved.

Two unidentified women's deaths from 1980. He only hoped he and Bonnie didn't end up crawling around in a shuttered old hotel like they had this past week. He had hated that.

The Cold Poker Gang meeting in the game room of the home behind him had been wonderful, his second with the special task force of retired detectives since he had left active duty and joined them. Last week he had been told that he and Bonnie would be partners and tonight the two of them had been welcomed to the meeting with a standing ovation by the other detectives for solving in just one week what seemed to be an impossible cold case.

Cavanaugh wasn't sure if part of the ovation was for the fact that neither of them had killed each other, since both of them had worked alone for a decade before retiring and were both known for being opinionated and very independent. More than likely there was a pool on which one of them would quit first. But as it turned out, he really, really liked Bonnie and had enjoyed every minute with her.

She was almost as tall as he was at just over six foot, in great physical shape, and had a smile that could light up a room. She had short brown hair that framed her thin face and deep brown eyes that he felt could sometimes see right through him.

After a week together, he actually wanted to spend a lot more time with her.

And for him, after years of working and being alone, that was saying something.

After they had gotten their second case from Andor, the retired detective running the cold case task force, they had decided to go get a snack and some coffee and read it over together, see what initial ideas they could come up with. So with about fifteen or so retired detectives still playing poker at the basement game room poker tables, Cavanaugh and Bonnie had waved goodbye and headed out.

The night was cool and both of them wore light jackets over their badges and guns, and by the time they reached his car parked on the street near a driveway full of cars, Cavanaugh was wondering if he should have worn a heavier coat. The high desert of Las Vegas could get bitterly cold in the winter at night. He just hadn't expected this level of cold tonight.

Bonnie had on dark slacks, flat dress shoes instead of her regular tennis shoes, and a white silk blouse under the dark silk jacket. Clearly she had felt that going back the second time to the Cold Poker Gang meeting had been a reason to dress up a little.

He liked how she looked normally, but tonight he had to admit that she was stunning.

He had even dressed up a little for the evening, putting on a brand-new jacket that fit him better than his older sports coats. His daughter Kathy had been working on him to not wear the old sports coats so much, but they were his style.

Suddenly from behind him Bonnie said, "Did you see that?"

Bonnie kept herself in good condition and liked to run and work out at the Las Vegas Athletic Club on Rainbow. But now, as he turned to ask what she had seen, she was already on her hands and knees on the concrete sidewalk in front of the house, looking under a black sedan parked in the driveway.

He had parked his white Cadillac just off the end of the driveway and he had no idea which of the detectives owned the sedan.

"Come here, little one," she said.

She clicked a few times and then rubbed the concrete in front of her, trying to coax something out from under the car.

He stood quietly, his breath fogging up the air, not saying anything, not wanting to spook whatever she was trying to get.

She got off her hands and knees and sat down on the sidewalk, leaning on her side, head still down almost on the ground, still talking softly to something under the sedan.

He was amazed she could do that so easily. She was fifty-eight and he was only a few years older than she was and also in great shape. But being on the concrete on his hands and knees or sitting like she was doing now was not something he wanted to try anytime soon. Not even on a gym mat.

And more than likely if he did try it, it would take two others to get him back to his feet.

At that moment, a black and white cat, very small and very thin, came out from under the car and up to Bonnie and dropped something from its mouth in front of her.

Bonnie scooped up the cat and gave it some scratches and rubbed its ears, talking excitedly to the cat, telling it how good it was, and calling it little momma.

He didn't move, but it was now clear that the small thing the cat had dropped in front of Bonnie must have been a kitten. Almost newly born from what Cavanaugh could tell from three paces away.

Bonnie talked to the mother cat like it could understand what she was saying.

"Do you have more babies?" Bonnie asked, putting the momma cat down and picking up the little one carefully, keeping her hands open to show the momma cat that the baby was safe.

Momma cat licked her baby once in Bonnie's hand, clearly not worried that Bonnie had it.

"Go get your other babies," Bonnie said.

As if the cat understood, she turned and trotted away toward the back of the neighbor's house. It was pitch black in that direction and the little cat disappeared almost instantly.

Bonnie stayed seated on the sidewalk right where she was, holding the little kitten in her cupped hands and just staring at it like it was the most precious thing she had ever held.

Finally she looked up at Cavanaugh, frowning.

"Momma cat is very thin, clearly starving, and this little one seems to be barely holding on as well. You got a box or towel or something in your car? We got to keep these guys warm."

"Towel and larger file box," Cavanaugh said, turning to his Cadillac sedan. He put the case file they had just been assigned on the back seat, then went to the trunk and dumped his financial tax files from last year out of a box there and secured them so they wouldn't slide. Those files were headed to his accountant and he could get another box.

Then he put the towel he used to cover a hot seat in the summer in the box, then got it over to Bonnie quickly.

She nodded thanks, not taking her eyes from the little baby cat in her hand. She was lightly breathing on it to warm it up.

He again stepped back to make sure that he wouldn't spook the momma cat.

At that moment, as Bonnie was putting the little kitten into the box in front of her, momma cat came back with another kitten.

She dropped the kitten next to Bonnie, who praised the momma cat and petted her for being such a good girl.

Cavanaugh stayed completely silent and still, watching Bonnie work her magic on this stray cat. A lot of things had impressed Cavanaugh about Bonnie after only knowing her for a week. And this was another.

She clearly had a way with cats.

And an empathy for caring for other living creatures.

Bonnie carefully picked up the other kitten and put it in the box with the first kitten, moving both to one side before showing that the mother cat should jump into the box.

The mother cat did and licked both kittens.

"Any more babies?" Bonnie asked the mother.

The mother cat didn't seem interested at all in getting out of the box to go get more kittens. In fact she turned around a few times before settling in on her side. Bonnie moved the kittens over closer to her.

Momma cat licked them some more, moving them in even closer.

To Cavanaugh, that was a clear signal that there were only the two kittens. And considering how thin and starving the mother cat looked, even two kittens born alive was amazing.

"We need to get them to a vet and quickly," Cavanaugh said softly.

"I agree," Bonnie said, staying seated on the sidewalk and guarding the box.

Cavanaugh moved backwards slowly to his car and then got around on the other side before using his cell phone to search for an emergency animal clinic that was open late and that dealt with cats. It was about nine in the evening so most vets would be closed.

He found two emergency vets that were open and called the closest one that was in Summerlin. They told him to get the cats in immediately and that they would be there waiting.

"Help is fifteen minutes away," he said to Bonnie as he clicked off his phone.

Bonnie nodded. "I'm going to pick up Momma cat and then the box. Leave the back door open on this side and be on the other side, but don't get in yet."

Cavanaugh understood exactly. He quietly opened the back door on the passenger side and then moved around to the driver's side, again standing very still.

Bonnie stood slowly, a feat that Cavanaugh marveled at, but said nothing. She picked up momma cat and then the box with the kittens, all the time talking softly to the mother cat.

She carried the box over to the car and put it on the back

seat, then put the mother cat into the box with her kittens and then moved in to sit beside the box.

Once again the mother cat just lay down, clearly happy with the situation.

Bonnie carefully closed the door.

Cavanaugh slowly opened the driver's door and then got in, closing the door softly.

"Seems you have found yourself some cats," he said, smiling at Bonnie.

"We have found ourselves cats, partner," she said, smiling back. "You can't get out of this that easily. Now get us to the vet before we lose all three of these little darlings."

He laughed softly and less than fifteen minutes later they had the momma cat and her two kittens in the vet's office.

And not for the entire time did Bonnie stop talking softly to the momma cat and petting her gently.

CHAPTER TWO

January 24th, 2019
Las Vegas, Nevada

Bonnie stood beside the vet examination table with the file box and kittens in it, not really believing what had just happened. She had managed to talk a stray mother cat into trusting her, letting her help with the kittens.

But the way the mother cat wanted attention and petting, it was clear she hadn't always been a stray. More than likely just lost and she was clearly starving. Completely amazing the two kittens had been born alive.

Cavanaugh stood beside her and back slightly so he wouldn't threaten the cat. Bonnie had really, really enjoyed her and Cavanaugh's first week together, far more than she had thought she would, and she had come, in a very short week, to really like and respect Cavanaugh.

Maybe even a little more than just like him. She found him attractive, actually. He was slightly taller than she was and in great physical condition. He often wore older sports coats to kind of hide how really smart he was, but tonight he had put on a new suit jacket over a custom shirt and slacks. He looked downright handsome.

And now, with his actions of being silent, being careful while she was trying to deal with the cat made her realize just how really smart and caring a man he was. How in the hell had she gotten so lucky to be partnered with him after all the years of being and working alone?

Around them the small examination room had two plastic chairs and a wooden coat rack against one wall that was covered in posters about different problems dogs and cats face. There was a white exam table sticking out into the middle of the room, and in the far corner was a white cabinet with a small sink and wall cabinets above it. A scale sat beside the counter next to a door that led into the back.

They both stood silently, Bonnie with her hand on the momma cat who seemed to almost be purring. More than likely this was the first time in a while this poor little girl had felt safe and cared for.

At that moment a young woman with a white coat came into the examination room. She was very short and tiny, and Bonnie and Cavanaugh both towered over her.

"I'm Doctor Kathy Jane," she said, extending her hand and smiling.

"Detective Bonnie State and this is Detective Cavanaugh," Bonnie said as they both shook the doctor's hand.

Bonnie liked Doctor Jane instantly. She had short, cropped black hair and wide, bright-green eyes and a smile that seemed to reach her eyes.

Doctor Jane turned to the box with the cat and kittens and her voice instantly went to soft and gentle.

"Well, little girl," she said to the momma cat, "seems you have had an adventure."

As the doctor picked up the momma cat, Bonnie said, "She just came to me, dropped one of her babies in front of me."

"She and her little ones need help and she knew it," the doctor said, holding the mother and giving her some pets, clearly a person used to handling cats. "Smart little girl. And very young. This is more than likely her first litter. And it will be your last," she said directly to the momma cat. "We'll worry about getting that taken care of later."

Doctor Jane looked at the momma cat for a moment, turning her to really check her out. "Clearly well-loved at one point. We'll get her some fluids and food and check a few of these scratches. Also get the mites out of her ears and get rid of the fleas. We will also check to see if she was chipped. Don't worry, she's going to be fine."

The doctor turned and pushed a button near the counter and a moment later another woman, also in a white lab coat and much taller than the doctor, opened the door.

The doctor handed the cat to the other woman. "Full treatment, but careful, she has just had kittens. Check for a chip."

The other woman nodded and turned, letting the door close.

"Now what do we have here?" the doctor asked, putting a white towel on the table and taking one of the babies out of the box and putting it on the towel, then put the other one on the towel before moving the file box aside.

Cavanaugh took the box and moved it back to the floor and out of the way without saying a word.

That was the first time Bonnie had actually really looked at the kittens in any kind of light. One was an orange tabby, the other almost pure black with what looked like a spot of white on its tiny paws.

Both were no bigger than the palm of her hand and barely moving.

The doctor took one look and then said, "Be right back."

She left the kittens on the table on the towel.

"Wow, are they tiny," Cavanaugh said, moving up to stand beside Bonnie to get a closer look.

"Yeah," Bonnie said. "Too tiny and not moving right. I kind of doubt that either one will make it."

She had seen newborn kittens before. Those were moving more, and were larger.

"Damn," Cavanaugh said. "That would suck."

At that moment the doctor came back in with a couple of eyedroppers and some fluid in a bottle that she was shaking.

She handed one eyedropper to Bonnie and then filled the one she had with fluid from the bottle and handed the bottle to Bonnie.

"We got to get some nutrition and fluid into these poor things or they won't last another hour."

She put the eyedropper down in front of the black kitten and pushed it towards its mouth, letting some fluid drip out as she did.

The baby took it and the doctor carefully let the baby drink almost one drop at a time.

"Go very slow," the doctor said, indicating Bonnie should do the same with the orange kitten.

Bonnie's hands were shaking as she filled the eyedropper and then eased it down, steadying her hands on the table and moving the dropper closer to the orange kitten. It took only a moment and the little kitten was taking in the fluids.

She couldn't believe she was doing this. In all her life, Bonnie never imagined herself as a caring type. Even with Jacob, her son, she hadn't been that great a mother, even going back to work on the force within a month after Jacob was born.

Now she was dropper feeding a newborn kitten. Not something training came naturally for.

After a long minute with both of them bent over the exam table feeding the kittens, the doctor nodded and stood.

"Let's give them a moment to rest, then give them a little more."

"What are we feeding them?" Bonnie asked.

"It's a powdered kitten milk substitute," she said. "Mostly water. They looked a little cold and dehydrated."

She handed the dropper to Cavanaugh, who looked stunned.

"Give them each another half dropper full," she said. "I'm going to go check on the mother, see if she is going to be able to feed them."

With that the doctor left the room.

Cavanaugh sort of looked at the dropper, then the kitten and shook his head.

Bonnie laughed. "Just keep your hand steady on the counter and let the kitten do most of the work."

He nodded and for the next minute they fed the two tiny kittens, who seemed to be gaining more energy by the minute.

And that gave Bonnie the sense that there just might be a little hope for them.

CHAPTER THREE

January 24th, 2019
Las Vegas, Nevada

Cavanaugh, in his wildest imagination, had not expected after his second time attending the Cold Poker Gang task force to end up dropper feeding a newborn kitten. He loved cats, always had. But this was not something he even realized it was possible to do.

Around him the veterinary exam room seemed almost too sterile and too small. The exam table extending out of the middle of one wall felt small and low. But for the last minute or so his focus had been on getting some fluids slowly into a tiny black kitten.

He and Bonnie had just finished with another half-dropper of formula for each kitten when the doctor came back in. At first glance, he had thought she looked like a kid, she was so short and tiny. But her face and wide green eyes showed this woman knew what she was doing without a doubt. And she carried herself as if she was in complete control, which at the moment she was.

And she clearly loved what she did, loved animals.

"Good news," she said, her voice bright, her smile wide. "The momma cat will be able to feed them. But it won't hurt if for a few days while momma gets stronger you also give the kittens some nourishment as well. At least through tonight."

As she was talking she picked up one kitten and gently rubbed its stomach for a moment, then did the same with the other. Cavanaugh knew that was to get the digestion moving a little in the kitten. Normally the mother cat would do that.

"Momma cat is not chipped I take it?" Bonnie asked.

"She's not," the vet said. "And I was right, she is very young. She and her kittens are going to need a comfortable and safe and warm place to stay. Indoors, with a cat box. She survived outside this time, but I don't think that little love of a girl is an outdoor cat at all."

Cavanaugh glanced at Bonnie, who was looking thoughtful. He knew exactly the place. His house had an attached apartment he hadn't even shown Bonnie on the times she had been there this last week. Mostly over the years he had forgotten it was even there. He kept it closed off from the rest of the large place because he sure didn't need the room and his cleaning people kept it dust-free every month. Heck, he had kept half of the main house closed off as well.

"I know exactly the place," Cavanaugh said.

Bonnie glanced at him.

He smiled. "Trust me."

"I think I got in trouble the last time a man said that to me," Bonnie said.

"I think I got in trouble the last time I said it," Cavanaugh said.

"This just might keep your streak alive," Bonnie said, winking at Cavanaugh.

Damn he liked being with Bonnie.

The doctor laughed and then put the kittens back the box, then turned for the door. "Momma cat should be ready to go in a minute or two. I'll get you a couple of small feeding bottles and enough formula to last you for a few days. You more than likely won't need to do it that long. And also some special soft and hard food for the momma."

"Thank you, Doctor," Bonnie said.

"Don't thank me," the doctor said. "It's going to be up to you two to keep these three alive."

With that, she left, pulling the door closed behind her.

Both Cavanaugh and Bonnie stood, staring at the closed door, letting what the doctor said sink in.

Then Bonnie turned to Cavanaugh and looked him right in the eyes. "You up for this?"

"I think so," Cavanaugh said, nodding. And actually, he felt he was. He loved cats and had even told Bonnie he had been thinking of getting a cat or two to make his big home seem less empty.

And Bonnie had told him that she loved cats as well.

"Are you?"

"I'm retired," she said, smiling. "I got the time."

He laughed. "Really good point."

"So where is this place I'm supposed to trust you about?"

"I showed you my house last week?" he said.

"Parts of it," she said. "It's huge and wonderful."

"Well," Cavanaugh said, "it's even bigger than I showed you. If you go through the family room where I watch television, there is a door that leads into a two-bedroom apartment. Private entrance on the east side and everything."

Bonnie just laughed and shook her head. "You have got to be kidding me."

"When Karen and I bought the place, we figured it would be a good secondary income. We furnished the apartment, had it ready, but when she got sick and then died, like a lot of the rest of the big house, I just closed the apartment off. Cleaning people keep it clean, but I don't think I have even been in there for years."

"You just keep amazing me," she said. "So you think the cat and kittens would be comfortable in there?"

Cavanaugh nodded. "Room to move around, cat box in the laundry room in there, food in the apartment kitchen area. And the entire thing is contained. I can close the door to my kitchen and open the door to the television room so they can have that space as well."

"That's a mansion for this little family," Bonnie said, looking into the box at the two kittens. "And it sounds perfect. Thank you."

"Means you will spend more time there with the care of these little ones," he said. "You all right with that?"

"Absolutely," she said.

And with that he smiled and went to stand beside her to look at the two tiny kittens that he hoped beyond hope that they could keep alive.

CHAPTER FOUR

January 24th, 2019
Las Vegas, Nevada

Bonnie couldn't believe the size of the apartment attached to Cavanaugh's home. It even had its own driveway on the east side of his home. She had thought that was a neighbor's driveway, actually, when he first brought her to see his place, and every time she had been here working with him in his dining room on the last case. But the apartment driveway went past his place through some trees to a sheltered parking area and a small circular drive.

Trees and some shrubs blocked the view to the main back-yard that Cavanaugh had shown her last week. Everything was done in low-water plants and the turn-around was in red brick.

His home was a sprawling ranch-style house with stucco siding and tile roof. It sat on a massive lot. Trees and shrubs not only gave it privacy from the street, but you could barely even see a neighbor's house. She loved it and could see why even after all the years of being alone since his wife had died, he hadn't sold the place.

He had told her that he and his wife Karen had just bought it and furnished the home when she got sick and then died. So he really didn't feel her in the place at all, which had allowed him to stay. They hadn't had the time to make it their home.

Cavanaugh pulled up on that apartment side of the house instead of in his normal driveway.

"From the main house you wouldn't even be able to tell anyone was parked back here," Bonnie said, shaking her head in amazement as she climbed out of Cavanaugh's Cadillac in front of what looked like a front door to a normal home.

"One of the reasons Karen and I initially thought we could rent this place out," Cavanaugh said. "Save some money on the mortgage."

"And all these years you never thought about renting it?"

Cavanaugh just sort of shrugged, which Bonnie was learning in only a week with him that he actually never had thought of it.

"Paid off the house when Karen died, had more than enough money at that point, so never really needed to put up with the problems renters would cause."

Bonnie nodded at that. She could understand completely. She had gotten divorced from her husband, mostly because of her job and his cheating. She had managed to buy a small one-bedroom high-rise condo not more than a half-mile away. But since her ex had left all his money when he was killed to her and her son Jacob, she understood how Cavanaugh could just keep the house out of sheer momentum. She was still in her small condo for the same reason even though she could now afford something larger and more comfortable.

But unlike her marriage, clearly Cavanaugh and Karen had had a great marriage at the time of her death. Now, even fourteen years after she had died, he still was just moving forward, not giving some things much thought.

And she didn't blame Cavanaugh at all.

The momma cat and her two kittens were riding in a cat carrier in the back seat, curled up on the same towel that had been in the file box. Cavanaugh and the vet had both agreed it would be safer to transport momma cat and the little ones that way, so Cavanaugh bought the carrier and all the food. Then they had stopped at a store and he had bought a cat box, some cat dishes for momma cat, and some cat sand while Bonnie stayed in the car and talked with the kittens.

Bonnie had paid the vet bill, Cavanaugh bought everything else. Turned out it was pretty even on the money that both had spent.

So at the moment the cats were officially both of theirs. They were brand-new partners for the Cold Poker Gang task force and brand-new partners in sharing three cats.

Bonnie didn't want to think about that too much at the moment. She just wanted to enjoy both.

Cavanaugh unlocked the door to the apartment and turned on some lights, and Bonnie followed him carrying the empty cat litter box and the bag of cat dishes. The apartment at first glance was amazingly large and felt very comfortable.

The front door entered into a massive living room with brown-toned cloth furniture that clearly had never been used. The furniture all faced a stone fireplace with a wood mantel. Directly ahead of the door was a large dining room and to the left a kitchen, also spotless. A hall led off to the right between the living room and the dining room.

The floors were some sort of light hardwood and the walls were painted a light tan. The dining room table was huge and made of oak. Six chairs surrounded the table and it looked like there was room for more. The appliances in the kitchen looked new, but clearly were dated. Not surprising since this place had been furnished just before Cavanaugh's wife died and then not been touched.

She was instantly comfortable here, just as she had been in the rest of Cavanaugh's house.

"How do you get into your place from here?" she asked.

"Through the kitchen there is an alcove to the left. Pantry shelves on one side, door into my television room on the other. Can be locked from both sides."

"Nice and hidden," she said.

Cavanaugh flicked on the hall light. "Laundry room is this way. I'm thinking the cat box would be great in there. We can block the door open."

He showed her the laundry room and she agreed. It was large and had a washer and dryer on one wall and a counter with cabinets on the other. The washer and dryer still had their original stickers on them and had clearly never been used.

He took the cat box from her and put it in a back corner. It seemed to fit perfectly, like the area was designed for it.

He then showed her a large master bedroom with two oak dressers and a massive king-sized bed. The master even had a decent-sized bathroom.

A second bedroom was across the hall from the master and next to the laundry room. A second small bathroom was between the laundry room and the living room.

A furnished, private two-bedroom, two bath apartment near downtown Las Vegas. This could be renting easily for twelve to fifteen hundred a month or more. Yet Cavanaugh just let it sit empty.

"We could put a couple blankets down in that corner," Cavanaugh said, pointing to a carpeted empty corner of the small bedroom, "and then take the lid off the cat carrier and put the carrier on the blankets there."

"Shut the doors on the master bedroom and the other bathroom," Bonnie said, nodding. "That will give Momma cat room to move into the main part of the apartment and to the cat box, yet keep her babies safe and warm in the back. I think she'll like that."

Cavanaugh nodded. "I'll get a couple blankets for here and get the cat sand and take care of that; you want to bring the young family in?"

She nodded. "You know you have an amazing place here."

He laughed. "Yeah, realizing that. Sort of seeing it for the first time in years. Actually seeing it, not just walking through it for some reason. Showing it to you is helping."

"Glad to be of service," she said as he opened a hall closet door and started to dig out a couple of extra blankets. "And thank you for doing this for the kittens. My condo is so tight, it would be tough to make this work."

He laughed. "Not lacking for room in this place, that's for sure. Glad I had it available."

She helped him get the blankets situated in the corner of the bedroom, making it a soft and fairly warm place for the kittens, then together she and Cavanaugh headed back out to the car.

He got the cat sand, she took the carrier.

"Come on, little ones," she said to the cats. "Let's show you your new, wonderful home."

And for the next hour they got the young family situated, showed momma cat the cat box, got her food bowls full, and let her eat and then explore some while they gave the kittens some more food with small bottles.

What an amazing evening and what a way to start their second week together as partners.

CHAPTER FIVE

January 24th, 2019
Las Vegas, Nevada

Cavanaugh could not believe how much he was enjoying being with Bonnie and taking care of the little cat family. He was so glad she had allowed him to be part of it, since she was the one who had coaxed the mother cat to her. He had thought about getting a cat or two for a long time, but as with most things in his personal life, he just never got around to it.

Now it seemed life sort of got him around to it. Life and having Bonnie at his side.

Momma cat was fed, the babies fed and looking better by the hour, and he and Bonnie were at the kitchen table in the main part of his house, both sipping on a glass of water. It felt very late, but actually it was just eleven p.m. The cats had only taken two hours from the time Bonnie saw the momma to having them settled in his extra apartment. Amazing.

"The doc said we need to feed the babies a little every few

hours tonight," Bonnie said. "Maybe tomorrow too until we are sure momma kitty is able to keep them alive on her own."

"I can handle it," he said. "I remember those kinds of days when Kathy was born."

"Yeah, same with Jacob," Bonnie said, shaking her head. "It was months and months before he slept through a full night. I actually don't remember much of it but a blur and being so tired I could hardly stand."

Cavanaugh laughed. "Thankfully we will only have a night or two with these little ones. We're both too old for much more."

"Hey, speak for yourself," she said, laughing.

He just smiled at her.

"So how about I take the first shift?" she said. "I'll get the new cold case file out of the car and read it for the next few hours, then feed the babies and head for home, if you don't mind me borrowing your car. You get four hours of sleep and take the next two shifts, getting some sleep between the feedings. I come back at seven for that shift so you can get a little more sleep."

He nodded. "Sounds very logical and won't kill either one of us completely."

"Exactly," she said, smiling. "Even at our *advanced* ages."

"I deserved that," he said, laughing. He stood and moved over to a drawer in the kitchen and got out two keys.

He held a round one up. "Here's a key to the apartment and this one is a key to this house, which also works on the door between the apartment and the television room."

She looked actually surprised when he slid the two keys across the counter to her, then got a second car key out of a drawer and slid it to her with the others. But she didn't say anything.

"Feels good to have someone else here in town have a key to

this place," he said. "The only other person with a key is Kathy and she's up in Seattle, so always worried me that no one else could get in here quickly if needed."

She nodded to that and put all the keys in her pocket. "Thanks for the trust."

"We're partners," he said. "I trust you with my life out there."

She laughed. "Yeah, good point."

CHAPTER SIX

January 24th, 2019
Las Vegas, Nevada

They unlocked the door between the apartment and the house, then Cavanaugh said good night and headed off toward the other side of the house, leaving her alone in the wonderful apartment.

Bonnie went out to the car and got the new case file, then went into the back bedroom to check on the kittens. Mother and babies were sleeping fine in the bottom part of the carrier.

Damn they were cute.

She so loved cats and couldn't believe she hadn't gotten one before now.

She took the case file to the apartment kitchen table. Sometime tomorrow she would buy a coffee pot for this apartment and some coffee and a case of bottled water.

And maybe a radio for some music.

She felt amazingly comfortable in the apartment. It had been a long time since a place calmed her and made her smile.

She wandered around for a few minutes looking and testing all the furniture, then with a glass of tap water she settled into reading, spreading out parts of the case file to keep things straight.

This case looked worse than the one they had tackled and solved last week. Two different women, one in the fall of 1979 and one in the fall of 1980, had been found in cars parked on the edge of Highway 95 outside of town. Both women had been killed somewhere else and their teeth destroyed and their fingers and thumbs cut off, so no way their identity could be traced.

Now there was DNA, but she didn't see anywhere in the file where DNA had been tried. Or even saved. At the time, 1980, it was still years ahead of when DNA was proven to be a good thing to use and twenty years ahead of when it became common practice in law enforcement.

Both women had been left dressed and staged behind the wheel of the car and neither had been sexually attacked.

The cases of the two women had been looked at over the years a number of times, thanks to the pushing of Metro Officer Matthew Young, the last being over a decade ago. Seems he had found the second body and had helped out on traffic with the first body in his first year on the job. He had made it his mission to try to keep the cases fresh, at least for a decade or so. More than likely he had retired and just let the cases slip into the past.

She had a few cases like that herself.

She had been just starting college in California at the time of the murders and had no memory of even articles about what had happened. Of course, back in 1979 and 1980, Las Vegas was still a small town and the mob still had fingers in many of the casinos. Likely the murders didn't even make it past a back page of the paper. No point in scaring away tourist money.

She looked through everything and discovered that, as of last report, Officer Young was retired and still alive living out in Henderson. Looked like he might be their first stop tomorrow.

That, and trying to figure out if they could get any DNA to be tested. Might not be possible after forty years. And who knows if the metro evidence lock-up still had much from these cases. Thirty-nine years was a long, long time.

At around one in the morning, she left the file spread out on the table for Cavanaugh, and then getting some of the artificial kitten milk in both bottles, she went in to disturb the little family.

All three looked like they were doing a lot better and momma cat let Bonnie give the babies a little food while she licked and bathed the one not being fed.

And the entire time momma cat purred.

Then when Bonnie was done with the kittens, she gave momma cat some fresh soft food on a small plate.

It only took Bonnie about fifteen minutes to feed the little ones, wash out the bottles and leave them for Cavanaugh, then head out, locking the door as she went.

It took her a little bit to adjust the seats in Cavanaugh's Cadillac, but she managed and thirty minutes later, totally exhausted, she had her alarm set and was crawling into bed for at least a few hours sleep.

Much, much needed sleep.

CHAPTER SEVEN

January 25th, 2019
Las Vegas, Nevada

Cavanaugh managed to stagger out of bed at three in the morning to give the little kittens some food. Missing a little sleep would be worth it to keep the little things alive.

But wow, getting up like that hurt. It had been a long, long time since he had had to get up in the middle of the night for anything. He had forgotten how really unpleasant it was.

Bonnie had the case spread out on the apartment's kitchen table and the two bottles for the kittens washed and waiting for him.

He made a little of the milk and put some in each small bottle, then headed back to see how the cats were doing.

Momma cat stood and stretched as he came in, talking softly. She was clearly happy to see him.

"Let's get you some food first," he said, putting the two

bottles on the towel next to her, petting her, and then coaxing her to come with him back into the kitchen. She did and he got her a fresh plate of soft food, petted her gently for a moment or two, then went back to feed the kittens while she ate.

He had just finished with the second one, the orange one, when momma cat came back in and crawled into the bottom of the carrier and started giving the kittens a bath.

"I'll leave it up to you now," he said, washed out the bottles, and was back asleep in ten minutes.

He did the same thing at five in the morning. The second time was even more painful, and this time momma cat wasn't very hungry. She just let him feed the kittens a little while licking them.

Then he went back to bed again. He couldn't even remember his head hitting the pillow.

He awoke around eight, a little past his normal time to get up, showered, put on a pot of coffee, and then went to check on the cats.

Bonnie was stretched out on the bed in the guest room, sound asleep. Momma cat was curled up against her. The kittens were looking very healthy and were asleep in the carrier.

Cavanaugh just sort of looked at the scene, drinking it in, enjoying it. Bonnie looked like she belonged here. And momma cat sure loved her, of that there was no doubt.

It looked like all of them had survived their first night together. When he first saw those kittens he would not have given odds on that happening.

He couldn't believe how much he had come to really like and admire Bonnie in just one week being with her. And maybe he was even falling a little for her, something that in the years since Karen's death he had never imagined possible.

He just shook his head and turned and went back to his kitchen. Both of them were going to need coffee and breakfast and it just so happened he had fresh bacon, eggs, and toast.

A perfect way to start off a new day with a new family of kittens and a beautiful partner.

CHAPTER EIGHT

January 25th, 2019
Las Vegas, Nevada

The rich, thick, wonderful smell of bacon and eggs woke Bonnie. At first she couldn't figure out where she was at, then she remembered stretching out on the guest bed in the cat room after feeding the little family and having momma cat jump up and stretch out beside her.

Momma cat was still there and Bonnie gave her some good petting. Then momma cat, purring, jumped down and got back into the carrier with her kittens.

Bonnie used the guest bathroom to splash water on her face and straighten up her hair before going in search of the source of that wonderful smell.

"Knock, knock" she said as she entered Cavanaugh's home from the apartment.

"Great timing," he said from the kitchen beyond his television room. "I was about to come and wake you."

"A corpse, which is what I feel like, couldn't sleep through this wonderful smell," she said going into the kitchen. "I am starving."

Cavanaugh had on what looked to be a new pair of jeans, expensive running shoes, and a blue dress shirt with the sleeves rolled up. He was standing in front of the stove clearly ready to fill two plates with food.

"Coffee there," Cavanaugh said, pointing to the large pot. "Cups in the cupboard above it. Poor me a cup as well if you wouldn't mind."

She did and took both cups to the table, then got silverware and some napkins for both of them as he put eggs, bacon, and fresh toast on plates. The smell was so good, combined with the fresh coffee smell, it was almost painful. Never had she remembered a kitchen smelling so good.

And being here with Cavanaugh felt so right.

Cavanaugh got the food in front of both of them at the kitchen table, sat down and they both ate in silence for a moment. She couldn't speak. She was savoring every bite of the food and every sip of the coffee.

Finally, between bites, she managed to ask, "How did it go for you?"

"Painful," he said. "But the cats were great. No problem."

"You were right. This parenting stuff is for the young," Bonnie said, laughing. "I have no memory of how I managed it."

"Better to forget some things," Cavanaugh said, "but a bumpy night sure makes food taste better."

"I was thinking these are the best bacon and eggs I had ever tasted."

"Didn't know I had that skill, did you?"

Bonnie laughed. "There's a lot of things I don't know about you. But looking forward to learning."

They ate in a comfortable silence for a moment, then Cavanaugh asked, "You got any ideas about the case?"

"Worse than our last one," Bonnie said. "You get a chance to look at it?"

"Not a bit," he said, "past the glance I gave it last night at the meeting."

"Two murders forty years ago," Bonnie said. "All identification of the victims destroyed, including cutting off their fingers. No idea if there was any DNA saved since it is a county case and because it was so far before DNA practices."

"Let's hope there's something in the evidence locker," Cavanaugh said.

Bonnie agreed with that. "It's a weird one. And something bothers me about it more than anything. The two victims were found a year apart, but in the same posed situation. That kind of thing usually means a serial killer at work, yet no more bodies were found."

"Yeah, weird," Cavanaugh said, finishing up the last of his toast and then sipping on his coffee.

"The patrol officer who found the second body and pushed on the case some might still be alive out in Henderson," Bonnie said, then also finished her wonderful breakfast.

"You think that might be a place to start?"

"I do," Bonnie said. "And then get Jacob doing some computer searches."

She was so proud of her son, Jacob. On their first case last week she had learned that not only was he a computer expert, but already had high-level security clearance with the city and worked on both local and state and sometimes federal tasks. He had been their eyes and ears and allowed them to be in the right place to capture that creep.

As Cavanaugh had said, the three of them made a great team. And even though she had always been proud of what her son had become, working with him and seeing him through Cavanaugh's eyes increased that pride to almost chest-busting proportions.

"So how about we spend some time going over the case together," Cavanaugh said. "Give the little ones a bit of food, and then call this retired officer to see if he'll talk with us."

"Sounds perfect," she said. She stood, took his mug and hers and refilled them. "And thank you for a wonderful breakfast."

"You are more than welcome," he said. "And it was honestly my pleasure. Cooking for someone else is always far more fun than cooking just for yourself."

"I agree with that," she said. "Only time I've cooked for someone else was when I got Jacob to come by for dinner. So in other words, damn near never."

Cavanaugh laughed and together they got the dishes into the dishwasher and with coffee cups in hand headed back into the apartment to work on their new case and check on their new little family.

Just about a perfect morning as far as Bonnie was concerned.

CHAPTER NINE

January 25th, 2019
Las Vegas, Nevada

Cavanaugh and Bonnie spent over an hour poring through the case together on the apartment's kitchen table, talking about details and mostly looking for holes that someone might have missed, or that the new DNA or computer world might be able to crack that wasn't available in 1980. There was no doubt they were going to need to go to the Metro evidence storage and see what might still be there for DNA sampling.

If anything. That was Cavanaugh's biggest fear about cases this old. Nothing would be left.

Cavanaugh could understand why these two cases had gone cold. No victim identity, no idea where the victims were killed or why they were transported to that location and left.

And why a year apart?

He knew that year meant something, but damned if he could come up with anything that made sense, other than a serial killer pattern that suddenly started and then stopped after only two victims.

And why be so concerned about the victims' identity not being discovered? Clearly the killer understood that if the victim was known, it would lead back to him or her.

"You know," Bonnie said, "if the location the killer left the cars was important, that is now completely gone. Covered by freeway and subdivisions."

"Yeah," Cavanaugh said, nodding as he looked at a map of the location where the cars were left. "Back then Highway 95 was a two-lane road leaving town at that spot. But now the city has expanded out over that area completely."

"We might want to have Jacob check when certain things were built or announced to be built along Highway 95," Bonnie said. "If this is a serial killer, the construction might have forced a change in the body dumping."

"And the new dump was never found," Cavanaugh said, not liking that idea at all.

"Exactly," Bonnie said. "And with the city expanding out along Highway 95, logical."

"Damn I hope you are wrong," Cavanaugh said. "I hope these are the only two victims."

"But you're afraid I'm right, aren't you?" Bonnie asked.

"Yeah," Cavanaugh said, looking at the details of the case spread out in front of him. "Because this being a serial killer is the only thing that makes sense."

Bonnie took a blank paper and made a note to Jacob about asking when expansion projects along Highway 95 had been announced.

"Might also have Jacob check the police arrests right after the second body was found," Cavanaugh said.

"Hope the killer made a mistake and was put away for another crime?" Bonnie asked, nodding as she wrote the note.

"We can only hope," Cavanaugh said.

And he really, really hoped that was what happened. Or that this killer was dead and would never be found. He would be fine with that as well.

"Well," Cavanaugh said after an hour or so, "time to see if Officer Young is willing to talk."

Bonnie dug his phone number out of the file and made the call. It seemed that retired Officer Young was more than willing to talk about the case and gave them directions to his home in Henderson.

"About an hour?" Bonnie asked the officer, then nodded. "See you then."

She clicked off his phone. "He's clear, very sharp, and excited we are looking at this case. He wants to help."

Cavanaugh indicated the file spread out in front of them. "Going to need all the help we can find."

"I'll call Jacob, tell him what's happening," Bonnie said. "See if he'll meet us for lunch."

Cavanaugh indicated the direction of the apartment. "Think the little family will be all right for that long, or do we need to swing back here?"

"I think we come back after talking with the Young, then go meet Jacob."

Cavanaugh laughed. "I think we're on the same page there. I'll gather up the file here, you get the food for the kittens ready."

As Bonnie stood, momma cat came out of the back, stretched, and then gave a soft meow.

"You hungry?" Bonnie asked.

Momma cat came over and rubbed against her and then as

Bonnie was dishing out some soft food, Momma cat came over to Cavanaugh and he gave her some scratches before she went to the plate of food Bonnie offered.

Cavanaugh was amazed that he was enjoying having a cat in the house so much. And even more amazed he was enjoying being with Bonnie even more.

He thought his life had changed last week. Seems that this week was bringing even more changes. And he was fine with that.

CHAPTER TEN

January 25th, 2019
Las Vegas, Nevada

The January day had turned clear and slightly warm. Bonnie enjoyed the ride with Cavanaugh out to Henderson. He drove smoothly and in control. It had been so long since she had actually been a passenger in a car, she was realizing she was seeing more than she normally saw when driving and paying attention to the road. She liked that.

And if she had to admit it, she really liked not driving. And Cavanaugh clearly enjoyed driving, so in their first week they had settled on using his car and him doing the driving and it had worked out great.

Henderson was a growing city expanding to the south of Las Vegas. In fact, it was already the second largest city in Nevada and showed no signs of slowing its growth, since it had a lot of room to expand.

It was mostly modern strip malls and expensive homes in

planned neighborhoods. Every neighborhood seemed to have a name. Officer Young lived in one called High Valley and the homes were clearly large and fairly uniform, with about five different basic styles. The trees and plants in the neighborhood showed that this wasn't a new development.

The Metro Police Force took care of all the area and cities around Las Vegas, making it one huge force, so the Cold Poker Gang task force could work in Henderson and the other towns in Clark County.

Cavanaugh found the home easily in the winding streets with the help of his GPS and Young met them at the door before they could even knock.

He didn't look to be much older than they were, although Bonnie knew he had to be at least a few years older. He carried himself like someone much younger and a smile lit up his face that made him seem even younger. His hair was gray and thick and he stood almost ramrod straight. He had to be almost her height.

The records showed that he had served as a Metro patrol officer for almost thirty-five years before retiring.

Bonnie had had some pleasant experiences working cases with the career patrol officers over the years. They were a combination of street cops, patrol officers, and detectives, all rolled together. And they almost always worked alone. She admired them a great deal.

They introduced themselves and Young said, "Just call me Young. Everyone does."

Young directed them into a plush but comfortable living room, decorated in brown tones and with a lot of family pictures on a fireplace mantle. From the looks of the pictures, he had two kids, a large number of grandkids, and a wife.

"Thanks for giving me a heads up that you were coming," he

said. "Since Barbara died I kind of let things go around here. Amazing how many pizza boxes and Coke bottles a guy can accumulate between the cleaners coming in."

"Your wife?" Bonnie asked, glancing at the pictures.

"For over forty years," he said. "Cancer two years ago and I just haven't had the energy to get my ass out of this big place and find something more suited to my needs, as my daughters tell me I should do."

"Oh, I understand that," Cavanaugh said, laughing. "My wife died almost fifteen years ago and I still haven't moved from the massive place I live alone in."

"And it is massive," Bonnie said.

"Closed rooms off?" Young asked.

"Large sections of the place, actually," Cavanaugh said, laughing.

All Bonnie could do was nod to that.

"So," Young said. "Cold Poker Gang task force is looking into those cold case murders of the women in the cars?"

"We are," Bonnie said. "Hoping you could help us."

"I was going to approach the task force years ago when I first heard about it forming," Young said. "Then got sidetracked with Barbara and everything. So really looking forward to helping in any way that I can. This case has haunted me since I was a rookie on the job."

"Certain cases can do that, can't they?" Bonnie said.

"Seeing those two women with their fingers and thumbs cut off and their faces destroyed is not something I will ever forget."

Bonnie just nodded to that.

"And having the cases go cold and unsolved had to not help," Cavanaugh said.

"Drove me nuts," Young said, laughing lightly to himself. "Barbara wouldn't let me talk about it, I got so obsessed. I even kept some of the evidence when it was going to be discarded twenty years ago. Figured DNA might help if I could get someone to look into it."

Bonnie damn near came out of her chair. "You rescued evidence?"

"I did," Young said, nodding. "Metro evidence department called me one day about twenty years ago and told me that the department was cleaning out old evidence boxes to get more room and asked if I wanted to store some of it. So I got it in the garage. Barbara hated that, let me tell you."

"Clothes?" Cavanaugh asked.

"With bloodstains," Young said, smiling.

"Well, hell," Cavanaugh said, laughing. "Looks like we are in business."

Bonnie could only agree with that. They had just caught their first break.

CHAPTER ELEVEN

January 25th, 2019
Las Vegas, Nevada

Cavanaugh got on the phone to Andor from Young's living room while Bonnie and Young went out to Young's garage. Retired Detective Andor was the connection to the Las Vegas chief of police's office and he was the one who checked out the cases for them to work on.

He was the one who had handed the case file to them last night and said, "Good luck."

"We're at retired Officer Young's place," Cavanaugh said to Andor when he answered. "Got some possible evidence items from the two murders you gave us that might have old DNA on them. How do we go about doing this?"

"He had some of it there?" Andor asked, clearly as surprised at the news as Cavanaugh had felt.

"He did," Cavanaugh said. "Saved it from being thrown out."

"I can send some of it through channels," Andor said. "Going to take some time, though. You think the evidence chain is broken on the stuff?"

"More than likely," Cavanaugh said. "Been in Young's garage for twenty years."

"Yup, broken," Andor said. "So get it to Jacob. He'll have ways to get what you need done quickly."

"Got that," Cavanaugh said.

Bonnie's kid was really amazing and even after last week surprised Cavanaugh at how much Andor trusted Jacob to help.

"And say hello to Young for me," Andor said. "Tell him I'm sorry to hear about Barbara and ask him if he's ever going to join the fun."

"The task force?" Cavanaugh asked.

"Been wanting him to join since he retired six years ago," Andor said. "That's why I dug this case out of the records; see if you two can convince Young to get back in the game. We could use a mind like his."

"We'll do our best," Cavanaugh said and clicked off his cell phone.

At that moment Young and Bonnie came back in from the garage through the kitchen carrying three file boxes all marked "Do not touch!"

"Andor said to say hello and that he was sorry to hear about Barbara," Cavanaugh said.

"And he told you to work on me about joining the task force, didn't he?" Young said, laughing.

"He did. Said that was why he dug this case out of the records."

"We'll see how this goes first," Young said. "What about DNA?"

"Evidence chain broken so no point in taking the vast amount of time regular channels would take."

"Jacob can do it," Bonnie said.

"That's what Andor suggested," Cavanaugh said.

"Now it makes sense," Young said, clapping his hands and then pointing at Bonnie. "Your son is Jacob Statethe boy computer genius."

Cavanaugh was glad to see Bonnie actually blush as she nodded. "I'll call him and see if he's up for meeting all of us for lunch."

"Tell him none of that Thai this time," Young said. "I'm still burping the last lunch we had."

Cavanaugh laughed at Bonnie's stunned look.

Then she said, "Is there anyone my son doesn't know in law enforcement?"

"I wouldn't count on it," Young said, laughing. "That son of yours helped get my oldest granddaughter into the computer department at UNLV. I think he even teaches one of her classes there."

"He does?" Bonnie asked, clearly even more stunned.

Cavanaugh and Young both laughed at that.

Then for the next hour the three of them worked through the boxes of evidence that Young had saved from the evidence room. And listened as Young told of his up close and personal experience of finding the second victim.

Cavanaugh was just glad it hadn't been him. That did not sound pretty, especially as a patrol officer just into his second year on the job. No wonder this case had stuck with Young for so long.

CHAPTER TWELVE

January 25th, 2019
Las Vegas, Nevada

Bonnie gave her son Jacob a hug when he came walking into the Main Street Station Buffet where the four of them were meeting. He looked like he normally did, jeans, a T-shirt, hair unruly with a baseball cap pulled down, and a backpack over his shoulder. He was as tall as she was, but scary skinny.

She had always called what he wore his perfect disguise. A nightmare for police trying to get a description. If he did something, all any witness would ever describe would be a college-aged kid with a backpack.

Around them the late lunch crowd talked fairly softly. The high ceilings and decorative wood and stained-glass on the windows kept the sound down, not counting all the large plants scattered through the massive dining room. She loved this place and was relieved that Cavanaugh did as well. Cheap, lots of choices, and pretty decent quality. Perfect for fast breakfasts or lunches.

And really perfect for meetings like this. The big wooden tables had enough room to spread out and the wait staff didn't constantly pester you.

"So, going another round with Mom?" Jacob asked Cavanaugh, sliding into one of the heavy wooden chairs beside him.

"Still alive," Cavanaugh said, laughing.

"And I see Mom has gotten you roped into this as well," Jacob said, smiling at Young. "Good to see you getting out of that house some."

"You've been talking to my daughter again?" Young asked.

"Granddaughter," Jacob said, giving Young a smile.

"More than I need to know," Young said.

"Judy is a natural on computers," Jacob said. "And fast and creative. Might be able to help us if we need it at some point."

Young really smiled at that. "Now that is great to know."

At that the waiter took their drink orders and they all headed for the food lines. By the time Bonnie got back, Jacob was already halfway through an entire plate of food.

"You forget to eat again?" she asked, sitting beside him.

"Can't remember," he said. "Got busy working a case for the chief. Just wrapped up this morning."

"You work for the chief of police directly?" she asked, feeling slightly stunned.

Jacob just shrugged. "Pretty regularly, when he calls."

Bonnie watched her son go back to eating while Cavanaugh joined them on the other side of Jacob.

"Something wrong?" Cavanaugh asked, glancing at her.

She just shook her head and went to work at her food. Her

own son just kept surprising her. She really, really needed to spend more time with him and try to pry out what he was doing. But getting information out of him even when with him was sometimes harder than setting up a dinner meeting.

Fifteen minutes later, after Jacob got back with a second plate mounded over, they finally got around to talking about the case.

Young told his story of the two bodies, then the dead ends they had already looked at in both the stuff he had and the official case file.

"So can you get us some DNA hits from the blood on the victim's clothing?" Bonnie asked Jacob. "Andor said to ask you since the chain of custody would be broken anyway."

"Sure," Jacob said between bites. "A friend can get me some familial matches quickly, which should be about all we need to start with. Maybe by tomorrow."

"That's fast," Young said. "You can do that?"

Bonnie was surprised at that as well. Cavanaugh and Young both looked a little shocked.

"Not worrying about chain of custody, and official tests, sure," Jacob said. "Basic DNA tests are getting quicker and easier by the month. And since everyone is sending off their saliva in boxes these days, the database is getting massive."

Bonnie just nodded to that. Things around DNA testing were changing and changing quickly. She just had no idea it could be that fast.

"So got a question for you," Cavanaugh said. "And no idea if this is possible to do or not. But the traffic ahead of those women's deaths coming into the airport couldn't have been that much in 1979 and 1980. Any chance there are still records of those flights and if we can get a list of names of women matching the victims' descriptions or ages who flew into Las Vegas in the week or so ahead of their deaths?"

Jacob sat silently for a moment, clearly thinking, a forkful of roast beef halfway to his mouth. Bonnie thought that maybe Cavanaugh had actually stumped her brilliant son.

Then Jacob slowly nodded and dropped his fork and took out a note pad from his front pocket and started scratching down notes that looked like a combination of math and ancient Latin.

"I think we can do better than that if I can get Judy to help me," Jacob said. "We'll not only match the ages and such of women flying into the airport in those periods of times, taking out any who don't match, but then we'll trace it back to missing person's reports in their origin cities to cut the pool down even more."

"From all over the country?" Bonnie asked.

Both Young and Cavanaugh were sitting forward, looking shocked.

"Sure," Jacob said, scribbling a little more into a notebook before putting it away. "Just a matter of setting up a program to track it all and weed all the information down. Digging that kind of information out of old records should be interesting as well, but luckily the FAA kept records on computers ahead of those years and I doubt they purge anything."

"You can get into the FAA records?" Cavanaugh asked, clearly stunned.

"And not get my granddaughter arrested in the process?" Young asked.

Jacob laughed. "All legal. I have clearance."

Bonnie just shook her head. Of course he did.

Jacob took another bite of roast beef, then glanced at

Cavanaugh. "Really good idea. You're starting to think like you're in the computer age."

"I think that was a compliment," Cavanaugh said, smiling.

Young just chuckled.

"Don't let it go to your head," Bonnie said, laughing.

"Too late," Cavanaugh said.

CHAPTER THIRTEEN

January 25th, 2019
Las Vegas, Nevada

After lunch, Cavanaugh and Bonnie went back to his place to feed the little kittens. Mother cat and family seemed to be doing great. Momma cat, or as Bonnie was calling her, Little Momma, got fed in the apartment kitchen and as she was eating Bonnie called the vet to see how much longer they needed to do the feedings, since clearly momma cat was also feeding them.

And thankfully the kittens were moving around now like real kittens, which just made Cavanaugh happy more than he wanted to admit.

"Just through the early evening," Bonnie said, repeating the doctor's words to Cavanaugh after she had described the condition of the momma cat and the kittens. "Then maybe intermittently tomorrow."

"So a full night's sleep tonight," Bonnie said after she hung up.

Cavanaugh was glad to hear that. "But I still could use a nap now."

"Same here," Bonnie said. "Mind if I curl up with momma cat on the guest bed in the cat room?"

"I think the little ones would love that," Cavanaugh said. "Give me about thirty minutes for a nap and I'll get some coffee going. See where the rest of this day is going to go."

"Perfect," she said. "Thanks."

With that she headed toward the back with momma cat following her. That just made Cavanaugh smile.

Thirty minutes later, feeling refreshed, he handed Bonnie a cup of coffee as she came into his kitchen from the apartment.

"You know that place is really nice," she said after she took a sip and then sighed.

"Cats can do that," Cavanaugh said.

"They can," she said, smiling as they both sat down at the kitchen table with the case file between them. "But I meant the apartment. It has a comfortable feel about it."

Cavanaugh agreed. "Always thought it did as well."

She pointed to the case file sitting where they had left it on the kitchen counter. "Any more thoughts on that mess?"

"Thinking from the other side, actually," Cavanaugh said. "Someone who could do that to those two women must have had a home or shop here in Las Vegas."

"I'm thinking more outside of town," Bonnie said. "A gunshot would be noticed in town, even back then. So I'm betting our killer had a place outside of town, more than likely with a shop and tools to cut off those fingers."

Cavanaugh agreed with that, but wasn't sure where that was going to get them.

"So why stage them like that?"

Bonnie shook her head and kept sipping her coffee.

"And why take the chance of renting a car," Cavanaugh asked. "That alone has been making me crazy. Young and the others who investigated this case got nowhere with the cars."

"Pictures," Bonnie said. "We have facial recognition now."

She dug through the file quickly, pulling out the two copies of the two fake driver's licenses. She stared at them for a moment, shook her head and then slid them to Cavanaugh.

"Not even the same guy," she said. Then she looked at the notes in the file. "Says the licenses were real, but lost here in Vegas six months before they were used. The owners of the licenses checked out."

"Dead end," Cavanaugh said.

"Agreed," Bonnie said.

"But I'm still stuck on why two and then stop."

Bonnie just nodded to that.

The idea that the killer didn't stop just kept echoing in his mind. But there was not one bit of evidence that the killer hadn't stopped, either.

Damn this case was frustrating.

CHAPTER FOURTEEN

January 25th, 2019
Las Vegas, Nevada

For another hour after the wonderful nap, Bonnie and Cavanaugh went over the file one more time, just to make sure there was nothing they had missed. They had moved the main file to Cavanaugh's dining room table, so they could leave it spread out, plus the boxes they had gotten from Young.

Both of them were jotting down notes on note pads, but it was clear that neither one of them saw anything Young or other detectives hadn't seen. She was about to suggest that they take a break and feed the little ones when Jacob called.

"On speaker with Cavanaugh," she said, answering and putting her phone down on the table between then.

"I got the DNA samples to my friend at UNLV and he should have some preliminary results tomorrow morning," Jacob said.

"Wow, that's fast," Bonnie said. "Thank you."

"Might not need it for anything more than confirmation, though," Jacob said. "I think I found the identities of your two victims."

That rocked Bonnie back in her chair and Cavanaugh said, "You're kidding me?"

"Your idea," Jacob said. "Right after lunch, Young's grand-daughter Judy and I set up the search of the FAA flight records for the times around those deaths. We matched approximate age and then added in a missed return flight."

Bonnie just shook her head. "Of course. Great thinking on the return flight."

"That was Judy's idea," Jacob said. "And it helped that forty years ago there were a lot less flights in and out of here."

"So how did you narrow it down from there?" Cavanaugh asked.

"Didn't have to," Jacob said. "There was only one woman who fit the description of the first victim who missed a flight home two days after the body was discovered. And only one who fit the description of the second one two days after the second body was discovered."

"Amazing," Cavanaugh said.

"Fantastic work, Jacob," Bonnie said.

"Couldn't have done it without Judy's help," Jacob said. "We're still digging into the two victims. The first was a woman by the name of Lynn White from Kansas City. Twenty-one when she was reported missing by her family five days after her body was found here."

"Why didn't the missing person's report get connected here?" Cavanaugh asked.

"From what we can tell from the very sketchy records available, no one in Kansas City knew she had come to Las Vegas. Same goes with the second victim, a Barbara Reid from Denver.

She was reported missing in Denver three days after she was to return. Again, no record of anyone knowing she had come here, so no report here filed at all."

"And without fingerprints and dental records," Bonnie said, "there was no chance the other cases would get connected."

"Seems like that is true," Jacob said.

"Was either woman traveling with someone else?" Cavanaugh asked.

"Not that we can see," Jacob said. "But we will keep digging on both and will know tomorrow for sure with the DNA if these women are the two victims."

"Fantastic job," Cavanaugh said. "One more search if possible. Can you look for any records of finding women's fingers over the years?"

"Another good idea," Jacob said.

Bonnie nodded. It was a logical idea that somewhere along the way a finger might have been found.

"Thanks," Jacob said. "I'll send you both pictures of the two women and more details. Expect that in a minute or so. And Judy and I will call Young and tell him as well."

Bonnie just felt stunned as she clicked off her phone. Modern computers and smart thinking just cracked a forty-year-old puzzle as to who those women were.

Now it was time to find the killer.

PART TWO

The Victims

CHAPTER FIFTEEN

January 25th, 2019
Las Vegas, Nevada

Cavanaugh just sat back, staring at the file and the boxes of stuff they had gotten from Young. It was all on and around his dining room table and Bonnie was sitting, stunned, mostly just staring at her phone on the table.

They had the identities of the two victims after almost forty years. That was something, and when confirmed, he was glad he wasn't going to have to be the one to tell the remaining families.

But now they needed to find the killer's identity. And if the killer had stopped or just changed where he or she was dumping the bodies.

Suddenly he knew he had a way of maybe figuring out if there were more victims.

"Why don't we have Jacob run the same flight information searches for a few years ahead of these two and a few years after?"

Bonnie blinked and looked at him. Clearly she had been focused on something and his questions broke into that focus.

She slowly nodded, then clearly understood what he had said. "More victims?"

"If the killer kept the same MO, which serial killers often do, then he or she might continue that yearly pattern set up by these two."

"God, I hope there aren't any more," Bonnie said, reaching for her phone.

Cavanaugh hoped the same, but his gut sense told him that someone who would do what was done to those two women wouldn't have stopped back then.

Bonnie got on the phone to Jacob, then said, "On speaker with Cavanaugh."

"Hang on," Jacob said. "Talking with Young. Let me link him into this call."

Cavanaugh just shook his head. He would have no idea how to do something like that.

"Okay, Mom," Jacob said. "Young is on with us and Judy is here with me."

Bonnie indicated that Cavanaugh should talk.

"Great work again," Cavanaugh said. "Just amazing."

Bonnie and Young both agreed.

"Thanks," both Jacob and Judy said at the same time.

"So now," Cavanaugh said, "the idea that there are more victims has bothered me from the start of this."

"Me too," Young said. "Just glad I never ran across any."

"So, Jacob," Cavanaugh said, "wondering if you and Judy might extend your flight records search a few years ahead of when the first victim was found, and for some years after the second victim."

"Same basic age of the woman?" Jacob asked.

"And no return flight with a missing person's report filed afterwards in a hometown?" Judy asked.

"Exactly," Cavanaugh said.

There was silence on the other end of the line, then Jacob said, "We'll call all three of you back in two hours."

Then he hung up.

"Well, that got them excited," Bonnie said, laughing.

"I'm just hoping beyond hope they find nothing," Cavanaugh said.

"And what do you think they are going to find?" Bonnie asked.

"A lot more possible victims," Cavanaugh said. "Ones we don't have bodies for."

Bonnie nodded. She clearly agreed, and that didn't encourage him in the slightest.

CHAPTER SIXTEEN

January 25th, 2019
Las Vegas, Nevada

Bonnie fed the momma cat in the apartment kitchen while Cavanaugh started on giving the two little ones some extra. Then she joined him, helping with the little orange one. Both kittens were looking almost healthy and they both wanted a little, but not much, which the vet said would be a good sign that momma cat was giving them more than enough.

Bonnie felt so comfortable in this apartment, it was amazing. She was starting to wonder if Cavanaugh would consider renting it to her. She needed to move from her small condo, had realized that for years and just never thought to even look for a new place. But now she had stumbled into an apartment she really loved, but since she and Cavanaugh had only known each other now for a week, would suggesting that seem too fast?

She had no idea, but with each passing moment in the apartment, she was falling more and more in love with the place.

After the feeding, they both went out to the Cavanaugh's kitchen and Cavanaugh made them each a cup of coffee while Bonnie called Andor and gave him an update and said that they would confirm the victims' identities tomorrow with DNA, so don't tell the chief just yet until they were sure.

She laughed at how Andor was just as stunned as she felt, finding out the names of the victims so quickly after forty years. She then told him what Jacob and Young's granddaughter Judy were working on. With that, all he did was swear softly and say, "Keep me informed."

"So," Cavanaugh said, "the way I see it, we have two things to decide before Jacob calls us back. First, what are we going to do about dinner? Second, what are we going to name the little family, now that it's pretty clear they are going to survive?"

"How about I buy us dinner at Lillie's in the Golden Nugget?" Bonnie said. "Been wanting some good Asian food and they have the best close to here. We can talk about cat names there."

"An offer I can't pass up," Cavanaugh said.

Twenty minutes later they were seated against a back wall in the plush, dark-wood interior of Lillie's. The sound of the few others in the restaurant was muted and Bonnie was glad they were early, so that they could easily talk.

The dark wood walls and columns and low ceiling of this restaurant sometimes made the place noisy, especially when the grills had loud, often half-drunk parties around them.

Since they were going to talk about the cats, on the way over Bonnie figured she might as well also ask Cavanaugh about her taking the apartment.

So after they gave their orders, she just blurted out what she was thinking.

"I love that apartment. Ever consider renting it to me?"

He sat back, smiling slightly. She hadn't known him long enough to get a sense of what that meant, exactly.

"I was kind of hoping you might be interested in it," he said.

She felt sort of shocked at that. "You were?"

He nodded. "Came to realize that the apartment is a really nice place, seeing it through your eyes and spending time there."

"That it is," she said.

"And you have said a number of times how you need to get out of your condo. Haven't even offered to show it to me, actually."

She laughed. "Not much to show, actually. That's the problem."

"And besides," he said, "since we are now partners in not only the task force, but in a young family of cats, you being there would make things fantastically easier."

She laughed at that. "It would. No doubt at all. And I would love it. But are you sure? We've only known each other for a week."

"Longer than I would have known any other tenant I might rent that place to."

She sat for a moment, then nodded and smiled. "I would love it."

And he smiled back. "Now, what to name the cats."

At that moment they were saved by the waiter bringing their food.

CHAPTER SEVENTEEN

January 25th, 2019
Las Vegas, Nevada

Cavanaugh couldn't believe how happy the idea of Bonnie taking the apartment in his place made him. Granted, he had only known her for a week now, but having her close by just pleased him, and when she wasn't close, he found himself looking forward to when she would return.

For a guy who prided himself over the last decade or so on his working and being alone, that was impossible to imagine. But it felt right. He liked everything about her, including her strength, her focus, and her sense of humor.

Plus, she had a huge heart that she showed with the kittens. Now if they could figure out names they both agreed on for the cats, things might be headed in the right direction.

Around them in the low-light dark restaurant, the sounds of others talking and laughing stayed low and no one was sitting close to them at all. He really loved this place, the feel of it, and the food, but hadn't come here often. It always felt like a place to come with someone else.

They both started eating and were just about to get back to talking about cat names when Bonnie's phone rang.

She glanced at it and said, "Jacob."

"Oh, boy, here we go," Cavanaugh said, mostly to himself. He was very worried about what this news might show. Someone who mutilated and staged those two women's bodies had all the signs of a serial killer. He just hoped beyond hope he was wrong about that.

Bonnie clicked her phone on speaker and said, "Both of us here in a restaurant. For the moment we can talk."

"Young is on the line as well," Jacob said. "And Judy is with me."

"Well, bad news?" Young asked.

"Yes," Jacob said.

"Real bad," Judy said.

Cavanaugh glanced up at Bonnie. Her eyes looked worried and guarded.

He just forced himself to take a deep breath as Jacob went on.

"There were no women that we could find who matched the description before the first one forty years ago," Jacob said. "But every year since there has been a woman of the same general age and look who has flown into Las Vegas from somewhere around the country, always alone, not made the return flight, and been reported missing in her hometown a few days later."

"And all at the same time of year," Judy said.

"Every year?" Young asked.

"Every year after the first two," Jacob said.

"When did it stop?" Bonnie asked.

"It hasn't," Jacob said.

Cavanaugh felt his stomach clamp up tight and he sat back.

Young said softly, "Son of a bitch."

Bonnie just sat there shaking her head slowly.

Cavanaugh didn't want to think about forty women being killed. That was just too much. But what he didn't really want to think about was that this killer was still active today.

And still getting away with it.

How in the hell was that even possible?

Over forty years?

CHAPTER EIGHTEEN

January 25th, 2019
Las Vegas, Nevada

Bonnie finally made herself get focused. She no longer cared that they were sitting in a restaurant. They had to catch this killer. And that was going to be her focus until they did.

"Jacob and Judy," she said. "Could you start taking this the next step for us? If we're not dealing with something forty years old, we have a lot more tools. So can you find out where the last five missing women stayed, get their files and all the women's missing person's files from the hometowns."

"Credit cards on the last five or ten women," Young said. "See if there are patterns. Rental cars, taxies, that sort of thing."

Jacob said, "Sure, we'll get on it."

"We're going to need to bring in an active detective on this," Cavanaugh said. "Bonnie and I and Andor will go talk with Detective Fawn. Get the chief informed of what you have found."

"Great thinking," Young said. "Fawn is a good one."

"We'll put together a preliminary data report on this for the chief and how we found what we did," Jacob said. "And we'll send you all the names and files of all the women as soon as we get the missing person's reports."

"Thank you," Bonnie said to Jacob. "We'll get this killer stopped and brought to justice."

"Damned right we will," Young said.

"Planning meeting in the morning for breakfast?" Bonnie asked. "I'm buying if you all come down to the Main Street Station."

"Nine a.m.," Jacob said. "We should have a lot of this gathered by then. I assume you all want it printed out."

"One set for me and Cavanaugh," Bonnie said and Cavanaugh nodded. "If you wouldn't mind."

"Yeah, me too," Young said.

"No problem," Jacob said. "And one more thing. Only one woman's finger has been found and reported with a case opened and no results. It was found in 1981 in your backyard, Cavanaugh. A neighbor cat was chewing on it. A neighbor who owned the cat turned the finger into the police. There was a search of your place, but it was empty and nothing was found."

"My place?" Cavanaugh asked, stunned.

"Yeah, afraid so," Jacob said. "The owners you bought the place from bought the house the next year after the finger was found. So maybe the owner before that. I'll send you their information. Might not be linked at all. See you all in the morning."

With that he hung up.

Bonnie put her phone away in her pocket and glanced at Cavanaugh, who seemed to be focused off into the distance, clearly stunned at a woman's finger being found at his home.

Then he shook his head and leaned forward and went back

to picking at his beef dish. "I think we might want to get a few experts at searching for human remains out to my place tomorrow."

Bonnie nodded. "But didn't you say you had the entire back-yard torn up and landscaped just recently?"

Cavanaugh nodded. "They would have found something I'm sure, if it was shallow, but never hurts to check. That's a lot of acreage and a big house."

"True," Bonnie said.

"You still want to move into the place?" Cavanaugh asked.

"Of course I do," Bonnie said. "But can't believe this killer was working right under our noses for our entire careers. That just pisses me off."

"No way for us to even know it was happening," Cavanaugh said. "Somehow those women got on a plane to Las Vegas without telling anyone. We find the reason for that, I bet we find the killer."

"The local authorities searching for the missing women must have known they got on a plane. That would be easy to track."

Cavanaugh shook his head. "Not really easy, but most departments would have the ability and the clearance. And if that was the case, then we would have been notified here."

Bonnie laughed. "And how many of those do we get a year from around the world?"

"Too damn many," Cavanaugh said.

Bonnie knew exactly what he meant. The department had to get thousands of missing persons cases coming in a year. Far too many to do much with any of them. And most solved in a few days, couples running away to get married, abused spouses trying to escape, young kids thinking Las Vegas was the promised land. The reasons people ran to Las Vegas were legion.

But very few of them ended up dead or remained missing.

"And after the first two, "Cavanaugh asked, "why did the killer change the way of getting rid of the bodies?"

"If this is still going on as Jacob and Judy suggested, that means somewhere in this area are thirty-eight women's bodies."

"We're going to find this psycho before there is another," Cavanaugh said, clearly slightly angry.

Bonnie nodded and went back to picking at her noodles. She could no longer taste them.

"How about we get some to-go boxes," Cavanaugh suggested. "Take this back to the apartment and heat it up later after our appetites return?"

"Perfect idea," she said. She forced herself to eat a little more, than pushed the rest away. She would be hungry in a few hours, she had no doubt, and that would be perfect then.

CHAPTER NINETEEN

January 25th, 2019
Las Vegas, Nevada

Cavanaugh had his Cadillac running and the air inside warming up slightly from the cool night air as Bonnie called Andor. Cavanaugh was still having trouble shaking the image of a woman's finger being found in his yard, even though it was years before he bought the place. That was a possible lead they had to follow quickly, maybe tomorrow.

It was only six in the evening, even though it was totally dark and felt later. They were parked in the Golden Nugget open parking garage on the second floor. The lights gave the place an orange tint and the freeway a block away filled the air with a low rumbling sound. It felt slightly creepy to Cavanaugh, but as good a place as any to park while they called Andor.

They had to get him on board and get permission to contact Detective Fawn. Or have him or the chief of police do it. He and Bonnie had worked with Fawn on their last case, actually their first case together, and both of them had liked her a lot. No doubt at all this case would need an active detective at times, since more than likely the last two missing women still had active and open missing persons cases on them somewhere.

And the task force had strict rules that they could only work on cold cases. An active detective had to take over when any case became an active case.

Cavanaugh, before he had retired and joined the task force, had served as an active detective on a number of Cold Poker Gang task force cases. And he had liked helping the task force and having the retired detectives helping him as well.

When Andor answered, Bonnie said, "Got me and Cavanaugh and we're about to ruin your evening."

"I knew I should never have put you two together," Andor said. "Am I going to regret just eating?"

"You might," Cavanaugh said.

"So what happened now?"

Bonnie quickly told him what Jacob and Judy had found and what they were putting together for the chief.

Andor just swore softly.

"We're going to need an active on parts of this," Cavanaugh said. "Think you can get the chief to assign Fawn to the active parts?"

Andor laughed. "She might kill all three of us for even suggesting it. But sure. I'll call the chief now. What's your next play?"

"Tomorrow morning meeting," Bonnie said. "Jacob and Judy are gathering data on the last five to ten missing women. And looking for patterns in all forty of them."

"Jacob is going to get us files and we're going to have a breakfast planning meeting at the Main Street Station buffet at nine. Young will be there as well."

"I'll see if I can get Fawn there for that," Andor said. "We're going to need as much help on this as we can get." Then he took a deep breath and said, "Forty women. How the hell did that get by us all these years?"

"We're going to find out," Cavanaugh said.

"Damn right. See you in the morning," Andor said and hung up.

Cavanaugh turned to Bonnie. "Looks like we are going to need a large table."

"Good," Bonnie said. "The more we toss at this, the sooner this sicko ends up behind bars."

"Or dead," Cavanaugh said.

"That would be better," Bonnie said, nodding. "A lot better."

PART THREE

The Search

CHAPTER TWENTY

January 26th, 2019
Las Vegas, Nevada

Bonnie had stayed at Cavanaugh's place in the apartment for a few hours after dinner before heading home to sleep. They spent time with the little cat family to get their minds back from what they had learned. Then the two of them worked on looking through every detail of the information they had on the first two women's murders while finishing up their take-out Chinese food.

Until they solved this case, she wasn't going to think about moving into the great apartment. That could come later. And thankfully, the kittens weren't needing extra food, so she and Cavanaugh didn't have to get up and down to feed the little darlings tonight.

The next morning, both Andor and Detective Fawn joined them for the planning meeting. Fawn was only five-two, and solid, with bright red hair, and clearly very strong for her fifty-five years of age. She had not been the slightest bit happy either to hear that a serial killer had been working their town for forty years.

None of them were.

Jacob had on his student look and Judy looked like she could be his sister. Same height, same color backpack, short brown hair, and brown eyes that saw just about everything.

She gave her grandfather a kiss on the top of his head when she got there.

The information Jacob and Judy had brought was amazing, and they were still digging. And missing person's files were still being sent on women from their hometowns.

Jacob said at one point that he doubted he and Judy had a tenth of the total information they could get on the forty women.

As Bonnie had suspected, there were two active missing person's cases filed in Las Vegas for the last two women who had gone missing. So Fawn had taken those two cases and said she would focus on them, far, far more than any missing person's case before.

From the summary of the information that Jacob and Judy had brought with them, it was clear that every woman got on a plane, alone, to come to Las Vegas. They had all stayed at Strip hotels, but seemingly never the same one. And they had gone missing before they had checked out.

What had really bothered Bonnie more than anything was that all forty women had traveled on exactly the same day.

October 10th.

Why that day? What was so special about October 10th? Being that precise on their travel clearly meant the killer knew them before they left their hometowns. Or at least had some sort of contact or influence with them.

Andor also had made a few phone calls and would have a

team headed to Cavanaugh's place to search for buried bodies. None of them thought it would turn into anything, but they couldn't let it pass. And he had two others searching the evidence storage for any sign of the finger to get DNA from it.

Bonnie could tell that the very idea bothered Cavanaugh a lot and it wasn't going to stop bothering him until he had an explanation for the finger, or at least confirmation it had nothing to do with this case.

From the breakfast planning meeting, Jacob and Judy went back to gathering as much information as they could and sending it to everyone, almost every hour.

Fawn said she was clearing her caseload to do nothing but work on those two missing person's cases and she would keep everyone informed on anything she had found. And she was available to help on anything anyone needed.

Andor said the chief of police had been informed and would offer any help any of them needed as well.

Young took the files he had been given and, with a hug from his granddaughter, headed home.

Bonnie and Cavanaugh went back to her future apartment with the cats.

They put the new files for the last ten women on the dining room table in Cavanaugh's home and then both of them sort of stepped back.

The dining room table was huge, but it was already half covered with files and the file boxes from Young's garage from the first two cases were stacked under the window.

All the files on that table represented twelve women, two for certain who had been killed and ten that were missing and presumed dead. Fawn had the files for two others.

There would be twenty-six more missing women's files coming.

"This is going to be massive," Bonnie said, just trying to wrap her mind around this much tragedy.

"I agree," Cavanaugh said. "I used to work with whiteboards to try to figure out how to organize leads when things got this large. I think I'm going to get a couple large boards."

He pointed to the two empty walls near the door into the kitchen and living room where they would hang.

Bonnie liked that idea. "I think that would help us find that one detail that will lead us to this killer. Might want to pick up some files and file crates so we can organize things."

He nodded and turned for the garage door. "I'll be back shortly."

She stood for a few minutes in the dining room, sort of just taking it all in, not even looking closely at any of the files.

Then she went through the kitchen and Cavanaugh's television room and into what would be her new apartment.

Momma cat greeted Bonnie with a soft meow and Bonnie picked her up and petted her, letting the purring cat calm her.

"You hungry?" Bonnie asked.

Momma cat was and Bonnie put her down, got her some soft food, and then went into the second bedroom to check on the kittens. They were doing great and she sat on the floor and petted them for a short time before Momma cat came back and crawled into the carrier bottom and started licking her babies.

Bonnie climbed to her feet and lay down on the guest bed, just staring at the ceiling, trying to put herself in the place of one of the women.

From what Jacob had said, all of the women were in their early twenties, all single. All were college grads and all were working a good job when they took the flight to Vegas and vanished.

Something else that Jacob said had really stuck with Bonnie.

He said that none of the women had told any of their friends or coworkers or family where they were going.

None of them, or at least not the ones Jacob had the files on. There were a lot more files to get. And not counting emails and such from the last ten to fifteen.

But why would that many women keep a Las Vegas trip completely secret?

Bonnie was about to get off the bed when momma cat jumped up and lay down in the crook of her arm, purring. Looked like she wasn't going anywhere for a few minutes.

She woke up when Cavanaugh shouted for her from the door to his place. She had needed that nap and she gave momma cat some pets to thank her for the suggestion.

CHAPTER TWENTY-ONE

January 26th, 2019
Las Vegas, Nevada

Cavanaugh, on the way back from the office supply store, had come up with a huge question. Clearly the killer had aged forty years. But the missing women had remained all about the same age.

That made no sense at all, and Cavanaugh told Bonnie that thought as they unloaded the car and then worked on getting the whiteboards on the wall in his dining room. The boards, once mounted, made the room even brighter. And made the dining room feel more like a work office, actually, even with the big table in the middle. He had moved a number of the chairs out and into the extra bedroom across the hall to get them out of the way.

Bonnie had agreed that if the killer started at twenty, he or she would be sixty now. Somehow a sixty-year-old person still had the ability to get a twenty-something young woman to get on a plane to Vegas without telling anyone.

So to Cavanaugh that detail made a relationship aspect a far more distant possibility. But what would get a twenty-something woman to board a plane on a certain date without telling anyone?

Cavanaugh had no clue, yet whatever the reason, it had worked for forty years with forty different women.

That just seemed impossible.

For the next hour, Cavanaugh and Bonnie printed up the new files that Jacob was sending them. By the time they were ready for lunch, they had files on thirty-four of the forty women, including the same files that Detective Fawn had taken because they were active. And they had each file in file boxes and labeled, one decade per box.

It was flat overwhelming.

They made a quick run to Subway for sandwiches, then came back and ate them while printing off the last six women's files.

"I think we use one whiteboard wall to make a table and list all the victims from the first to the most recent last October," Bonnie said.

Cavanaugh had already thought of that. "With each victim we give age, job, hometown, hair color, interests."

Bonnie nodded. "And Las Vegas details as well with each name, where they stayed, rental car, how long they were scheduled to be here, that sort of thing."

Cavanaugh nodded. "And airline. Maybe we get all this on one board and we can start to pull some patterns."

"Or at least places to start digging," Bonnie said. "I'll do the writing. I can print very neatly and in small letters."

Cavanaugh laughed. "Hoping you had that ability."

He quickly started to line off each board with a thin black tape while Bonnie organized the files in order of dates, starting forty years back.

They had put two four-foot wide whiteboards together on one wall and two boards on another wall. The wall closest to the living room would be the master wall with all the women's names on it. He did twenty lines per board going across. Once he got all the horizontal lines on the first board, Bonnie started printing each woman's name.

When she got done with the first twenty women, she put the last file back in the box. "None of these first twenty women were married or even had a fiancé. A couple had boyfriends and almost none of them much of a family to speak of."

Cavanaugh nodded as he finished the last horizontal line on the second board. "I'm betting that holds as a pattern."

"So another mystery," Bonnie said. "How did our killer find women who were not in a serious relationship?"

"Maybe by promising them a relationship?" Cavanaugh said. "You know, secret love and all that?" He didn't much like that idea, but it tended to be at least a possibility.

"That would mean on these early ones our killer traveled to the women's hometowns," Bonnie said. "No email or internet back in those days."

Cavanaugh stopped lining the board and glanced at Bonnie. "Maybe pen pals?"

"Maybe," Bonnie said. "Nothing would surprise me about this case."

She went back to writing names on the second board as he worked on figuring out how many vertical categories they were going to need. He had no idea, so he just looked at the ten or so factors they already had and added in three more, which was about as many columns as he could get on one board anyway.

It took them another thirty minutes before they were ready to start adding information to the boards.

They started with age and hometown. Cavanaugh read off the name, the age, and where the woman was from, and hair color. After about ten, they decided to delete the hair color column, since it was clear there was no pattern.

On the early missing women, it was sort of stunning how little information they had. They had age, hometown, when they got on the plane, when they were scheduled to leave. Nothing much else.

On the last ten they had a lot more, including hotel information.

As Cavanaugh was going through the files and giving information to Bonnie, it dawned on him that they were missing one bit of information on their board.

"On that last column, put where the body was found."

Bonnie nodded and added that, then under the first two she noted where the two women had been found and how.

Cavanaugh stared at the empty column for all the other women.

"Where are they?" he asked more to himself.

"And why did the killer stop displaying the bodies?" Bonnie asked.

Cavanaugh looked at Bonnie, who was staring at the wall of whiteboards with the forty women's names on it. Then he said what he was thinking.

"It's against pattern for a serial killer to change that much. Maybe the killer didn't stop displaying them. He just stopped displaying them in Las Vegas."

"Shit," was all Bonnie said.

CHAPTER TWENTY-TWO

January 26th, 2019
Las Vegas, Nevada

Bonnie knew instantly that Cavanaugh was right. And thirty seconds later she had Jacob on speaker phone.

"I know you are crazy busy," Bonnie said. "But Cavanaugh had an idea as to what happened to the other victims. Would it be possible to do a search for Jane Doe's who were found in cars without fingers and teeth in other cities?"

"Great thinking," Jacob said. "We'll need to develop a search for that, but it is possible. I'll let you know the moment we find even one that matches."

He hung up.

Cavanaugh just shook his head. "Your son is amazing."

Bonnie laughed. "Yeah, the idea of searching through that many police databases over that many years looking for that kind of specific detail is mind-numbing for us poor mortals."

They went back to slowly filling in what details they could on the boards for each woman. The idea of doing this so they could both see it and see the patterns was a good one, with this much data.

One pattern that quickly started to emerge was that the women were scheduled to be in town only for five days. They all came in on the exact same day and all but one was scheduled to leave five days later on the 15th of October.

Another pattern was starting to form on the later ones. Most of the women were lower income. All lived alone. A couple had had domestic incidents with a family member or boyfriend that the police got involved with. Clearly not the types of women who would just fly off for a five-day vacation in Las Vegas.

When Cavanaugh mentioned that, Bonnie made a note to try to figure out how the women paid for the trips and where they got the money. That might be possible to check on the last five or ten. Bonnie would see if Fawn was chasing that detail or not.

Thirty minutes after Bonnie had called Jacob, he called back and she put him on speakerphone.

"Nothing," he said. "The two that were left in cars forty years ago is so unique, there is nothing close to that kind of thing in any city within a two-day drive of Las Vegas."

"So all the women are still here somewhere," Bonnie said, softly.

"Looks that way," Jacob said. "Sorry."

"Thanks for doing the search," Cavanaugh said.

"That's what we are getting the big bucks to do," Jacob said. He laughed, then said, "Talk with you two tomorrow."

"Night," Bonnie said before Jacob hung up.

"Well damn," Cavanaugh said. "We have a serial killer who changed pattern after the first two."

"Or is displaying them in a different way that hasn't been found yet."

Cavanaugh said nothing to that and Bonnie flat didn't want to think about that being a possibility.

Bonnie just stared at the board and at all the women's names. Impossible to even imagine that many lives cut short. Or maybe they weren't cut short. Maybe they were alive.

Not likely, but they needed to keep all possibilities open.

"Do you think there is any chance any of these women are alive?" Bonnie asked.

Cavanaugh looked up at the board, then shook his head slowly. "The pattern was set with the first two forty years ago. The pattern holds every year after that. They are all dead. We don't know why or how, but they are dead."

"But where are they?"

"There is a lot of desert out there," Cavanaugh said. "And basements. Somewhere in that mass of information is a clue that will lead us to the killer and where the women are."

Bonnie nodded. But more than anything she wanted to shift her focus to looking for a place where thirty-eight women's bodies might be. She had no desire to find it or see it, but she just knew that was the key to stopping this killer forever.

CHAPTER TWENTY-THREE

January 26th, 2019
Las Vegas, Nevada

After they got every bit of the information they could find in quick searches through all the files onto the whiteboards, it was starting to get late. But Cavanaugh felt hungry and far too wound up to sleep yet.

"You up for a late snack before calling this a night?"

Bonnie smiled, something neither of them had done much today. "I would love that. Let's get our little cat family some food first."

They got momma cat fed and the kittens some petting before they bid the cats a good night and climbed into his Cadillac. It was actually only nine in the evening, but to Cavanaugh it felt much, much later. He had on a light cloth jacket and it wasn't enough for the cold desert air.

"Someplace with hot chocolate and pie," Bonnie said,

rubbing her hands together as he got the car started and headed out.

"Ever been to Madge's?" he asked.

She shook her head and looked at him as he got them headed toward the downtown area.

"Little hole-in-the-wall diner a block off Fremont. Booths from the 1950s, milkshakes that could send you into a diabetic coma, and pie that tastes like it was made in heaven."

"I am so there," she said, laughing. "But going to skip the milkshake tonight. You think it's still open?"

"Seems to be always open," he said.

And it was. He didn't come in here that often, but every time he did it seemed the same woman wearing a name tag that said, "Madge" was the only one in the place. As normal, she had on a too-tight 1950s carhop dress and chewed gum like she was in a fight for her life against the gum.

The place itself looked right out of the 1950s, with red vinyl booths, green Formica tabletops, and a 1960s bubble-style jukebox against one wall playing oldies at a level that allowed people to talk. Signed and framed pictures of everyone from Elvis to Sinatra to President Kennedy filled the walls along with old 45 records. A couple of them were even signed to Madge herself.

There were two other couples in the diner and Bonnie led them to a small booth near the door away from the other couples while staring open-mouthed at the décor.

"You know, this town constantly surprises me," she said. "You would have thought I would know about a place like this."

Cavanaugh laughed. "Problem is just knowing about it causes weight gain."

"Hey, Detective," Madge the waitress said as she dropped a

couple napkins on their table. "You having your usual. Vanilla shake and large burger and fries?"

Cavanaugh laughed, amazed at Madge's memory and treating him like a regular even though he didn't come in more than once a month or so.

"Switching out the milkshake for a hot chocolate tonight," he said. "And this is my partner, Detective Bonnie State."

Madge chewed her gum even harder for a second, then smiled. "Nice meeting you Detective. You must be Jacob's mom."

Cavanaugh damned near rolled out of the booth laughing at the shocked look on Bonnie's face.

"I am," Bonnie said. "And I'm starting to wonder if there is anyone in this entire city my son doesn't know."

"Oh, I remember him," Madge said, laughing, "because every time he comes in I swear I'm going to make my rent. That kid can eat. And he told me once his mom was a detective, so I just put the name together is all."

"Impressive," Bonnie said. "And I'll have what Cavanaugh is having, plus do you have cherry pie?"

"Best in the city," Madge said. "Ice cream on it?"

"No other way," Bonnie said. "Even on a cold night."

"Got that right," Madge said, giving Bonnie a wink.

Madge then turned for the kitchen, saying something to one of the other tables on her way.

"This place is amazing," Bonnie said.

"Perfect way to relax after a day like today," Cavanaugh said. "And wait until you taste the food."

And Madge didn't let him down. The burger was perfect, the hot chocolate amazing, and he even went for a piece of pie of his own after tasting Bonnie's.

And even though it felt great to get away from the case for even a short dinner, he just couldn't pry his mind away from the finger found in his yard. And what they might find tomorrow morning in the search he had called in.

CHAPTER TWENTY-FOUR

January 27th, 2019
Las Vegas, Nevada

When Bonnie arrived at Cavanaugh's the next morning a little after eight, four police vans were already out front and it looked like the search of his yard had been going on for some time.

Cavanaugh was standing on his back patio, his arms in the pockets of a heavy ski parka. It was cold enough this early in the morning in the shade to see his breath in white clouds. The day was supposed to be in the high 50s, eventually, but it was a long ways from that this early.

As she got closer she could tell he was looking very worried. She would look just as worried in the same situation.

"Anything yet?" she asked.

"Nothing," he said. "Cadaver dogs are working the yard and ground-penetrating imaging has already covered most of the area. They started in the crawl space under the house and that was clear."

"Wow, that's fast," she said, watching the crew of six people and three dogs moving methodically over and through the backyard plants.

"They've been here since dawn," Cavanaugh said. "But makes no sense that one finger would be found and nothing else. So I've spent a little time this morning talking to my neighbors along the street, learning more about this area than I ever imagined I needed to know."

"Anything worthwhile?"

Cavanaugh shrugged. "Nothing but some rumors of an old mob boss living three doors closer to downtown, but he died eight years ago from old age. And that this area back before I bought the house used to have a large pack of feral cats. Seems the cat that had the finger wasn't the neighbor's cat, but one of the feral pack. Or that's what one neighbor said. Finding that finger is like an urban legend in this neighborhood."

Bonnie nodded. "Feral cat packs used to be all over the valley back when I was newer on the force and still on patrol. I seem to remember the city had a major campaign to trap them and find them homes back in the nineties."

Bonnie remembered being very happy when the city did that. She always felt like she needed to save all the wild cats she saw. And she saw hundreds almost every day back then.

Cavanaugh nodded. "One of the neighbors said a guy who lived three doors to the east of here fed the feral pack every day. He was also running a small cat breeding operation in his home of a rare breed of cat called a Korat."

"Never heard of the breed."

"Neither had I," Cavanaugh said. "Supposed to be rare and out of Thailand was all the neighbor told me. She said the guy was a doctor of some sort and kind of creepy, but sure loved cats."

Bonnie nodded. "A feral cat back forty years ago has a woman's finger and we're working on a case where two women are missing their fingers in that same time period. Seems a little too much to be a coincidence, don't you think?"

"That's what is bothering me," Cavanaugh said.

"Did you talk with the neighbor who fed the cats?"

"Moved a long time ago, house occupied twice since then, now vacant and for sale."

Bonnie glanced at Cavanaugh. "Think the real estate agent would show us and some cadaver dogs a house?"

"Damned good idea," Cavanaugh said, suddenly moving toward one of the men working in the yard. "I'll talk with the crew here, see how much they have left to do."

He handed Bonnie a slip of paper from his coat pocket. "That's the address and real estate agent's name. Call Andor to get a search warrant. We want to do this right."

Bonnie nodded. "Should I call the real estate agent to meet us as well?"

Cavanaugh nodded. "We're grasping at straws here, but might as well have her bring what history of the house she has, then get Jacob to do a search of the owner of the house back in that time frame."

"The feral pack did have a woman's finger," Bonnie said. "Not that distant a straw to grab at."

"Yeah, I suppose," Cavanaugh said.

She knew he had a point. This was a crazy long shot. But sometimes long shots paid off, and in a gambling city, she had learned that lesson far too well over the years.

And she knew Cavanaugh had as well, which was why he was going along with it.

She headed into the apartment to say hello to the three little ones and make the calls where it was warm and she might actually be able to feel her fingers again.

CHAPTER TWENTY-FIVE

January 27th, 2019
Las Vegas, Nevada

By the time the team of white-suited technicians and cadaver dogs gave Cavanaugh's property a clean bill of health, Andor had a search warrant for the empty home down the street. And the real estate agent was on the way to meet them.

Cavanaugh could not believe how relieved he was at having his home clean. Especially now that Bonnie was going to move into the apartment.

But that finger had to have come from somewhere. Maybe the murderer just tossed the fingers to the feral packs of cats while driving by. It would be a great way back then to get rid of the evidence. Hungry cats would make short work of something like a decomposing finger.

Or maybe there had been something more going on back then. Cavanaugh doubted they would find anything in an empty house that had been occupied twice since the finger was found. But it sure never hurt to look.

Now, his hands deep in the pockets of his ski jacket, the heaviest coat he owned, he walked beside Bonnie up the paved street he had driven more times over the years than he could count. But he honestly couldn't remember the last time he had walked it. Walking made the neighborhood seem so alien, actually. The old trees seemed larger, the houses had more details, the landscaping more flaws.

Behind them the cadaver dogs were being taken care of, given a rest, and the vans would be moved up the street shortly.

Around them the neighborhood was quiet, as it was every morning at this time. The few people that worked were already gone and the few kids that lived on the street were long off to school. Cavanaugh wasn't sure how many kids actually lived on the street. He seldom saw any at all, that he could remember.

The older trees towered over the street, giving it a lot of shade in the summer, but on a cold winter's morning like this one, Cavanaugh would have been happier with a little of the sun getting through.

The house they were headed for was also built the same time as the rest of the neighborhood, in the mid 1950s and was a sprawling sand-toned ranch house on a lot as large as his. At some point the front and side yards had been converted to low-water landscaping with gravel, cactus, the large original trees, and flowering desert plants.

He had driven by this house thousands of times over the years on his way to and from work and never had given it much of a look. It was just a neighbor's house, one that nothing ever seemed to happen in. And it clearly seemed to have been maintained, otherwise he might have actually noticed it.

And he had never met any of the owners. Of course, the

owner who had fed the feral pack of cats had moved long before Cavanaugh bought his house. In fact, he could never remember seeing a cat running lose in this neighborhood.

As they got to the house, a brown Lexus sedan pulled up and stopped, and a woman got out dressed in light blue sweatpants and a matching jacket. She had long brown hair pulled back tight and no make-up at all. She looked to be about five-foot even and not an ounce of fat on her and she moved quickly, like she was in a hurry. Cavanaugh guessed her to be in her mid-twenties and very successful, but he could have been off on that age guess by a decade.

Bonnie introduced them both and shook the woman's hand. Both of them just towered over the realtor.

"Teresa Hold," the woman said. "Nice meeting you, detectives. This property is my listing, so sure hope nothing is wrong. Just got some interest in it, actually."

"Thanks for coming out on an early Sunday morning," Bonnie said.

Cavanaugh glanced at Bonnie. Until that moment he hadn't realized it was Sunday. Typical when he was on a case, he lost all track of time or what day it was. Karen used to sometimes kid him about that, when she wasn't mad about it.

Teresa just waved the thanks off. "This job, like yours, is twenty-four seven. You would be surprised at the time of day or night I have sold homes."

Cavanaugh laughed and Bonnie nodded.

"We are working a very, very cold case," Bonnie said to Teresa. "We're looking at a time back in the 1980s or so and wondering what you have for records on the house from that time. Back in the days when the owner of this house fed a pack of feral cats."

"Wow, that does go back," Teresa said. "And there were packs of feral cats? Didn't know that."

Cavanaugh revised his age of Teresa back to her late twenties.

Teresa turned around and got a large file out of her car and handed it to Bonnie. "Everything I got in the records on the history of the house."

Cavanaugh looked over Bonnie's shoulder as she thumbed through the file.

The guy with the cats turned out to be the second owner of the home. He lived here from 1978 to 1990. A man by the name of Loch Woldstad.

Nothing else about him. Just information on the house and the condition at purchase and at sale. And that Woldstad had paid cash for the place.

As the search team vans pulled up in front, Teresa went up the front sidewalk and unlocked the realtor lockbox and got out a key, then unlocked the front door and pushed it open before turning and handing Bonnie the key.

"Just make sure everything's locked up and put the key back in the lockbox when you are finished. I assume you have a warrant so I can tell the owners."

"We do," Cavanaugh said, again revising the age of the agent back upward. No young agent would think of asking about the warrant.

"Thank you, Teresa," Bonnie said.

"Wish I could stay and watch the fun, but got a Pilates class."

She passed the first of the cadaver dogs on the way to her car, giving them a wide birth. From the look of worry on her face, Cavanaugh could tell she was clearly not a dog person.

CHAPTER TWENTY-SIX

January 27th, 2019
Las Vegas, Nevada

Bonnie was worried about what they were going to find in this sprawling ranch house, even though two other owners had lived here in the thirty years since Loch Woldstad's time. The large amount of years that had gone by on this case was the one thing that she just couldn't get her mind around.

That and the number of possible victims.

Bonnie also couldn't get past the fact that a woman's finger was found in this area in the same time period that two women were found with their hands cut off. That was just too hard a connection to let go of just because Cavanaugh lived in the same neighborhood.

One of the three dogs and his handler went into the house as she and Cavanaugh watched from the front yard. The other two dogs started a search pattern of first the small front yard, working around the side of the house quickly.

Bonnie had worked numbers of times over the years with cadaver dogs. They were amazing. They could smell human remains up to fifteen feet underground and through concrete and could distinguish between animal remains and human remains with an amazing degree of accuracy.

So if there were human remains in this home or around it, anywhere, the dogs would find them. She honestly didn't know what to hope for.

She glanced at Cavanaugh and he just shrugged. Neither of them seemed to know what to do while they waited, so they just stood in the front yard, hands in their coat pockets, staring at the house and the quiet around them and trying to stay warm.

She wasn't sure how much time had passed as they stood there silently, when one of the technicians working with the dogs came from around the house and moved to the truck.

"The dogs may have some hits," the tech said, a medium-height man in a white environmental suit that covered almost all of him except a round opening showing his face.

He pulled out what Bonnie knew was a ground-penetrating radar machine and quickly wheeled it toward the back, and Bonnie and Cavanaugh followed.

She was shocked at what she saw when they went around the back corner.

The backyard was a patch of grass, mowed perfectly, with flowerbeds along a back fence. A wild area of desert plants and older trees lay beyond the fence. It was clearly part of the property. Some owner in the past had put in a small, regular grass backyard, more than likely for a child since there was a children's swing set to one side of the yard.

Tiny red flags on wire stands were sticking out of the area just beyond the fence. The flags seemed to be in two rows spaced evenly apart, and there had to be over ten of them. And as they watched one of the dogs got another hit and another flag was put in the ground.

The flags were looking like cemetery headstones.

"Oh, shit," Cavanaugh said.

Bonnie felt her stomach twist into a knot. This couldn't be possible.

One of the dogs clearly found something again and the handler put another red flag in the ground. Again it looked like it was in a row with the other flags.

"If this is what I think it is," Cavanaugh said, "and this has to do with our case and not something else, Woldstad lived here from 1978 until 1990, so that means there shouldn't be this many bodies."

"The 1979 and 1980 women's bodies were in the cars," Bonnie said, "so nine or ten bodies depending on when during the year he moved. And assuming this is our case. Maybe he cut up the bodies?"

"Fourteen flags so far," Cavanaugh said softly.

The tech with the ground-penetrating scanner started to carefully work the area near one of the red flags. After a moment of staring at a screen, he turned to Bonnie and Cavanaugh and nodded.

"Looks like we might have a body about six or so feet down, wrapped in something."

Bonnie glanced around. She had to move and move quickly or they were going to be in trouble.

She shouted to the two handlers and two techs in the back-yard, "Listen up, everyone."

All the handlers and techs stopped and turned to her.

"This has to stay very, very quiet until we catch whoever is behind this. No radio calls, nothing that could be over-heard by the press. And you tell no one but your boss. We can't have this discovery getting out in any way. Understand?"

Beside her, Cavanaugh was nodding. "We'll get patrol out here to seal this site. And you are going to need tents."

All the handlers and techs were nodding.

"Get what help you need in here to recover what you are finding," Bonnie said, "but extreme caution and quiet on this. We'll make some calls and get the ball rolling."

At that the dogs and handlers went back to what they were doing.

"Oh, is Detective Fawn going to hate us for sure, now," Cavanaugh said, shaking his head. "But good thinking on clamping a lid on. This gets out and we lose whoever buried these bodies for sure."

"That she is," Bonnie said, actually feeling sorry for what they were dumping on Detective Fawn. "Paperwork on this will be through the roof. But I need to call her and get her here now."

"Agreed," Cavanaugh said.

Just as Bonnie was about to call to Detective Fawn, the dog handler who had been in the house poked his head out of the back door and said, "Detectives, need you in here."

"Oh, shit," Cavanaugh said again.

And with that, Bonnie could only agree. All she could think was, "Now what?"

CHAPTER TWENTY-SEVEN

January 27th, 2019
Las Vegas, Nevada

Cavanaugh flat hated how this was going, but felt relieved at the same time that they just might be making headway. They might, thanks to a feral cat thirty years ago, have caught a break.

On the way into the house, Bonnie called active Detective Fawn and told her she needed to be here, that it looked like they might have found a body dump. Cavanaugh could hear Detective Fawn swearing as Bonnie hung up, smiling.

Detective Fawn was named Isadora Fawn, but no one called her by her first name and lived to tell the tale. Fawn stood all of five-two on a good day and had bright red hair and green eyes. She was fifty-five years old, but she acted much younger. And she worked alone, just as Cavanaugh and Bonnie had both done the last ten years on the active force.

Cavanaugh liked Fawn a lot and respected her even more. And he knew, as a fact, that the paperwork she was going to have to do because of this find this morning would bury her for days. Cold Poker Gang task force members didn't do paperwork if a crime got solved by them. The credit and the paperwork went to the active on the case.

And Cavanaugh loved it that way.

As his eyes adjusted to the dimmer light inside the home, he could see the place had been updated to look modern. A brand-new kitchen was to his left and beyond a large living room with modern tile on the floor. Nothing of the original charm of this house seemed to be left at all beyond the look of the outside.

"This way, detectives," the tech said, leading them to a door that opened up into a staircase that went down.

"These houses seldom had basements," Cavanaugh said. "So this must have been added later."

"More than just the basement was added," the tech said.

Downstairs was what looked to be a large family room or what could be used as a game room. The basement was fairly deep so the ceiling was unexpectedly high. This was a nice addition for a large family, that was for sure.

The cadaver dog and his handler were on one side facing an empty built-in shelving unit that seemed to be custom made of oak.

"Body behind that," the cadaver dog handler said, pointing at the shelf.

At that moment the tech with the imaging device came down the stairs and joined them.

They all stood back as he worked, then after a moment he said, "There's a room back there, a fairly large one, from what I can tell. Got furniture in it as well."

Out of habit, even though there was little chance of any kind of trace left from the owner who built the room, Bonnie and Cavanaugh took off their coats and then both put on gloves and started carefully looking for a switch that might trigger a door.

The cadaver dog and his handler and the tech went back upstairs, with Bonnie reminding them both to keep this quiet and not put anything out over the radio at all.

They worked in silence for the next ten minutes, having no luck at all finding any kind of release on the shelf.

"Andor and the chief have slammed a lid on this discovery," Fawn said from behind them as she came down the stairs. "And Bonnie, your son is trying to track where the owner of this house moved to."

"Good to hear," Bonnie said, turning around.

Cavanaugh turned to see Detective Fawn dressed in jeans, an expensive green blouse, and a heavy winter coat. She shrugged off the coat and put it with their coats at the foot of the stairs, then came over to the shelf to join them in the empty room.

"Tech filled me in that the dogs say there is a body back there."

"We have spent the last fifteen minutes looking for a release on the shelf," Cavanaugh said. "Nothing."

Fawn stood back and stared at the large shelf, then she turned around and went back to the staircase. The railing was made of the same expensive wood as the shelf, as were the runners on the stairs. Clearly built at the same time.

"This guy would not have wanted anyone to find that room, right?" Fawn asked.

"Not if he left a body or two in there," Bonnie said.

Fawn was right, this wouldn't have a normal secret-type entrance that someone could stumble on. This guy had to feel certain the room would never be found, even if the shelves were taken out at some point. So chances were behind the shelf was just a regular wall. And that meant there had to be another way in there.

Fawn ducked under the stairs that had a storage area built in and clicked on her flashlight, looking around inside.

Then Cavanaugh heard a click.

"One of you want to take some photos of this for me?" Fawn asked.

Bonnie ducked down with her phone out and took some pictures of the back of the storage area wall slightly open.

After a few photos Fawn pushed it completely open and Bonnie took some more photos.

"What's with you two, always finding underground hidden rooms and tunnels that I got to crawl into?"

Cavanaugh actually laughed at that. Last week they had found a hidden room and tunnel in the basement of an old shuttered hotel and Fawn had had to crawl into that.

"Sorry," Bonnie said, turning and smiling back at Cavanaugh.

He had to admit, it was funny. But not to Fawn.

"Slants up like it's going up to the crawl space under the front part of the house," Fawn said. "You two are going to owe me a new pair of jeans if I ruin these."

With that Fawn disappeared into the tunnel.

And Bonnie ducked down into the area under the stairs and followed her.

Cavanaugh just stared at the small space and the tunnel where Bonnie and Fawn had disappeared. Crawling around under old hotels and now old houses was just not what he retired for.

Not in the slightest.

CHAPTER TWENTY-EIGHT

January 27th, 2019
Las Vegas, Nevada

Bonnie flat hated old tunnels and anything underground. Hated it, but she sure wasn't going to let Fawn go into this alone. There was just no telling what was under here.

Around her the walls of the upward slanted tunnel were wood, as was the ceiling and the floor. It was like she was crawling through a long, wooden box. Nothing at all creepy about that, considering they were looking for a way into a room with a possible body.

"Tell Cavanaugh to stay where he's at," Fawn said from ahead of her. "Two of us in here is more than enough."

"I heard that," Cavanaugh said from behind them. "And thank you."

"You owe us both dinner for this," Bonnie said.

"Deal," Cavanaugh said.

"That was easy," Fawn said as she reached the top of the slope. "Should have asked for more."

"Oh, it will be an expensive dinner," Bonnie said.

"I heard that as well," Cavanaugh said from down the wooden tunnel.

The tunnel opened up into what was clearly a crawl space under the house, but beside the light from Fawn's flashlight and Bonnie's light on her phone, there seemed to be no other way in or out.

And the ground was covered with a black plastic that more than likely served as a moisture barrier. Nothing about the crawl space smelled of mold or anything. In fact it had a dry smell and during the summer it must have been very, very hot in here.

"Dogs said all this was clear because they checked it from above," Bonnie said.

"Good to know," Fawn said.

She turned and the two of them moved along the wall toward the hidden room side of the basement, the black plastic making a cracking noise as they moved. Bonnie felt like there was a fine gravel under the black plastic. Small rocks, not large enough to pierce through the thick plastic.

The space was tall enough for them to move along on their hands and knees and finally they reached the other end of the basement wall.

"Doesn't seem far enough to have a hidden room space," Fawn said and Bonnie agreed.

"I think we just went the length of the basement to the shelf," Bonnie said.

"So the hidden room is under there," Fawn said, pointing to what looked like just more crawl space under the house, covered with a plastic tarp.

"So how the hell did anyone get into the room?" Fawn said, looking around.

Bonnie was wondering the same thing. And if this room was used by a serial killer, taking bodies in and out the way they had just come in would be almost impossible.

"Got a hunch," Bonnie said, "we just found an escape route."

"Feels that way," Fawn said, turning and crawling along the side of the basement room where the shelves would be. Then she hit something and stopped.

"Gravel under the tarp feels thinner here."

Bonnie moved up and using her phone as a flashlight shined it on the area as Fawn pulled back the tarp and brushed the gravel aside to show a wooden plate with no handle.

"Emergency exit," Fawn said, nodding. "Opens from the other side."

"So we haven't found the main entrance."

She shined her light around the area that more than likely would be on top of a secret room. The outside wall looked like it had a fireplace on it, with a foundation that went solidly into the ground.

"Fireplace," Bonnie said.

Fawn nodded and indicated that Bonnie should go back the way they had come.

"If we can't find something on the fireplace and have to break into the room, we're going through the shelves, not in this space," Fawn said.

"Very glad to hear that," Bonnie said.

"And I think Cavanaugh owes us two dinners each for this," Fawn said.

"Oh, trust me," Bonnie said, laughing as she crawled back toward the wooden tunnel. "He's paying."

CHAPTER TWENTY-NINE

January 27th, 2019
Las Vegas, Nevada

Cavanaugh watched nervously as Bonnie and Fawn made their way up the wooden chute and to the area under the house. He could barely hear them talking as they got deeper into the crawl space, and then after what seemed like an eternity, they came back.

Bonnie came down first and Cavanaugh helped her out of the space under the stairs, then Bonnie turned and helped Fawn.

Both women looked hot, but except for some dust on their hands and knees, not much worse for wear. He was just really glad they wanted him to stay behind.

"Some sort of emergency exit from the ceiling of the room on the other side of those shelves," Bonnie said. "No way in from up there."

"What did it look like under the house?" Cavanaugh asked.

"Standard crawl space," Fawn said. "Gravel base, black

heavy-plastic vapor barrier on top of the gravel. Pass any inspection without a second look."

"Dogs would have sensed a body buried under vapor barrier from the room above," Bonnie said.

"So, we check the fireplace in the room above this," Fawn said. "And if that fails we get techs in here to tear down that shelf."

They all grabbed their coats and Cavanaugh followed the two detectives back up the stairs and into the big, open area on the main floor of the house. The floor was a light tile of some sort with a faint pattern in it. The walls were all plain and painted an off-white. Light blue tile with a faint pattern covered the fireplace that filled the back wall, right over the secret room.

Bonnie went to the right side, Fawn went to the left side, Cavanaugh got on his hands and knees in front of the fireplace to look for anything that might be a latch or switch or something out of place.

After a minute of none of them saying a word, Fawn finally said, "Got it."

Cavanaugh and Bonnie moved around to where Fawn was on her hands and knees, pointing up under a ledge that looked to be a decorative extension of the hearth of the fireplace.

She reached up and pushed something and there was a clear click. But nothing happened.

Fawn stood and took hold of a decorative mantle extension that went around the fireplace and pulled.

Cavanaugh was shocked when the entire end of the fireplace swung open like a door and the dry smell of mummified death hit them.

"Pictures," Fawn said, staring at the opening, but Bonnie already had her phone out and was taking pictures from all angles.

Fawn glanced back at Cavanaugh and Bonnie, then turned for the opening.

"Techs need to go in there first," Cavanaugh said. "Might be trapped. I would put nothing past someone who could build this sort of hidden room and leave a body or two in it."

Fawn stopped, then stepped back and nodded. "You're right."

She stepped aside to go talk with the techs that were outside.

Cavanaugh stepped to the opening behind the fireplace and shined a light from his phone down into the hole to the room below. Just a metal steep staircase and a concrete floor was all he could see.

And the smell was clear, one that he had smelled many times over the years. Mummified human remains. Heat and time and extremely dry desert air did that to bodies and it had a distinct, dusty smell that was impossible to forget.

Cavanaugh was very, very glad that at the moment he wasn't climbing down into that hole.

Very glad indeed.

And he had no doubt that they had just solved a bunch of very cold missing person's cases.

Now they had to find out where this Loch Woldstad had moved to. And find out what he did with the next thirty years of bodies.

PART FOUR

The Discovery

CHAPTER THIRTY

January 27th, 2019
Las Vegas, Nevada

After an hour of watching the techs get set up at the house and clear the basement room, they got yet another shock of the morning. The woman who died in that basement was on a hospital bed. The room itself looked like a hospital room straight out of the late 1980s. And everything was clean, not one fingerprint on anything.

The woman on the bed had mummified from the heat and all the years of dry air, and she had a medical chart, on her chest, seeming clutched in her arms.

Bonnie's head was spinning now. The woman's name on the medical chart matched the woman who had vanished in 1989. That meant she died here before Woldstad sold the house in 1990. And Woldstad just left her with a medical chart.

Fawn showed them the chart. "Says she died of pancreatic cancer, basically natural causes. January 3rd, 1990."

"She flew in on October 10th, 1989, and vanished," Bonnie said.

"And then there was this down there on the wall, covered by a picture," Fawn said. She showed them what looked like a list of graves, with names on each grave and a date. Nine of the names Bonnie recognized from the names on the whiteboard back at Cavanaugh's, the others she did not.

"You think these are the names of the women buried out back?" Cavanaugh said.

"What I think is this entire case is just screwed up beyond words," Fawn said.

Outside the techs were getting a tent set up over the red flags. There were eighteen flags, all in two rows just beyond the fence line of the backyard.

And the flags matched the pattern of the picture.

Fawn sent Jacob a copy of the picture to get him started trying to figure out the other names.

And it was going to take hours for the techs to get the first body up from the back because they had to sift for clues in every bit of the dirt. So Bonnie and Cavanaugh said goodbye to Fawn and headed back up the street.

It hadn't warmed up that much, even though it seemed like it should have. It felt like an eternity that they had been in that death house, but in reality they had only been there for just slightly over two hours. It wasn't even ten in the morning yet.

They walked in silence back up the street to Cavanaugh's home and her new apartment, once she got moved in when this case was over. She loved the feel of this neighborhood and Cavanaugh's home and she wasn't going to let some killer from thirty years ago ruin that.

If the guy even was a killer. It would take some time but she had a hunch the autopsy of the woman on the bed would show that she had died of natural causes. Of cancer.

So what about all the others buried in the back?

And what the hell had happened to the two found in the cars. Was that something totally separate?

Once inside Cavanaugh's house and out of their heavy coats, they both went to check on momma cat and her little ones. Momma was very happy to see them and get more food in her bowl and it lifted Bonnie's mood to pet the little girl and her two darling kittens.

Then they went into the dining room.

Bonnie took a black marker and moved to the column where they marked the location of the bodies found.

"I think we can safely assume," Bonnie said, "without too much fear, that these eight women are buried behind that house."

Then she put "basement room" beside the name of the woman on the bed.

"So who are the rest of the bodies out there?" Cavanaugh asked. "Did he come back after he sold the house and keep burying more? Or do we have more victims during those first ten years?"

Bonnie nodded. "So on our list, victims one and two in 1979 and 1980 were left in cars with mutilated bodies. And victims 1981 through 1988 may be buried in the backyard. Victim from 1989 was in the basement."

"That still leaves thirty victims we have not accounted for," Cavanaugh said. "And maybe the extra bodies in the backyard."

That just made Bonnie shudder, but at least they were a lot farther along than they had been this morning. And nine more families would finally get closure.

"So where did Woldstad go?" Bonnie asked, more to herself than Cavanaugh who was standing staring at the board.

She called Jacob and put him on speaker so Cavanaugh could hear.

"Woldstad flat vanished," Jacob said without even a hello, as if he had been reading Bonnie's mind from a distance.

"What?" Bonnie asked.

Cavanaugh turned from the board like someone had pushed him and stared at the phone.

"Totally vanished," Jacob said. "He ceased to exist on the day after his house closed and he got the money in 1990."

"We know he stayed in the area," Cavanaugh said, "if he was responsible for what we found this morning."

"We are scouring bank records for deposits that match the amount of cash he got from his house sale," Jacob said. "And searching driver's license databases for images that match the photo he had on his Woldstad license. Nothing so far, including in the medical field in case he really was some sort of doctor."

"How wide an area?" Bonnie asked.

"When he didn't pop up instantly, we expanded the search south to Flagstaff, out into California, and north to Reno and Salt Lake. Anywhere that is an easy drive from here."

"Okay, shout when you find him," Bonnie said.

"Oh, you'll hear it without a phone," Jacob said. "And we are starting a search in the same time frame as the first victims for more missing women because of the other bodies in that backyard. I'll let you know."

With that Jacob hung up.

"Woldstad vanished completely," Cavanaugh said. "Now that I didn't expect."

Bonnie just stared at the board with its thirty missing

women. She had not expected that either. And she had not expected that there might be even more.

Not one bit.

CHAPTER THIRTY-ONE

January 27th, 2019
Las Vegas, Nevada

They spent the next hour in Cavanaugh's dining room they had converted to a war room looking at every detail they could think of, including what Fawn had sent earlier about the two newest cases that matched the pattern, the two they had the most information about.

All the names on the board just kept begging for explanations, but nothing seemed to be in sight.

Cavanaugh had this nagging feeling they were missing something right out in the open, and Bonnie did as well, but neither one of them could figure it out. And it was driving them both crazy.

Finally they made a call to Young and he was having the same feeling.

So Cavanaugh suggested the three of them get together and have lunch at the Main Street Station Buffet. They all needed to eat and maybe a good, old-fashioned brainstorming session between three old-fashioned detectives might uncover what they were missing.

In thirty minutes they all had food and were eating and Cavanaugh and Bonnie spent the next thirty minutes giving Young more details about what they had seen in Woldstad's house. Including the possibility that the woman on the bed in the basement might have actually died of natural causes.

Around them the noise of the buffet was just background, with tourists talking, dirty dish carts rattling past, laughter from a distant table echoing off the high ceilings.

"I'm guessing he put in the basement and secret room without any kind of plans for the remodeling," Bonnie said. "So that would be a dead end."

"Happened all the time back then," Young said, nodding.

Cavanaugh agreed. Vegas had still been a pretty small town back in 1979, and building codes were more like wishes than mandated rules.

"So it's killing me how we missed this sicko for all the years," Young said. "And how did he get all those women to travel on the same date and without really telling anyone where they were going?"

"And who are the extra bodies in the back?" Bonnie asked. "We won't know more on them until at least tomorrow, if then."

Suddenly it dawned on Cavanaugh the detail they were missing, and why they had gone to that house in the first place.

"Cats," he said.

Bonnie looked at him with a puzzled look.

"My neighbor told me the guy who was feeding the feral cats, Woldstad, also had a small cat-breeding operation going for a rare breed of cats called Korat."

Bonnie instantly had her phone out and had Jacob on the line.

Without even a hello she said, "Search for a cat breeder in this area who is an expert in the Korat breed of cats."

The three of them waited, their food forgotten. Cavanaugh just sat there, almost holding his breath. Could this be the detail they had missed?

Bonnie put the phone on speaker and sat it down on the table.

After a moment Jacob said, "Nothing. Why?"

"Because Woldstad supposedly bred them," Bonnie said, "when he was in his house where we found the bodies this morning."

"Give me and Judy ten minutes," Jacob said, "we'll search some databases, cat groups, and so on, and set up a search on the internet for the name. Spelled K-o-r-a-t, right?"

"I think so, yes," Bonnie said.

Cavanaugh nodded. He had looked it up on his phone for a minute earlier this morning. Very rare breed of cat originally from Thailand.

Then Cavanaugh thought of something else. "And as a hunch, you might want to search the emails of the last two missing women for that cat breed name and any kind of contact with someone about Korat cats."

"And also the women's health records, if you can get them," Young said.

"And if they were in abusive relationships of one sort of another," Bonnie said.

Cavanaugh looked at Bonnie and she just shrugged. Clearly they were all just tossing things against a wall hoping something would stick.

"You thinking sick, abused women came here to pick up a cat?" Jacob asked.

Cavanaugh and Young both laughed.

"Rare cat," Bonnie said, "and it's more than we have at the moment."

"Back with you shortly," Jacob said and the phone went dead.

Cavanaugh just shook his head as he stared at the phone.

"Something has got to stick," Young said. "We're running out of things to throw at the wall."

"We're running out of walls," Bonnie said and Young laughed.

For some reason, though, Cavanaugh no longer thought they were missing anything.

CHAPTER THIRTY-TWO

January 27th, 2019
Las Vegas, Nevada

Bonnie and Cavanaugh and Young had just finished lunch and Young had just got back with a piece of apple pie when Jacob called back.

"Might have a few details to toss into the mix," Jacob said. "First off, the last five women who went missing all were lower class and mostly broke, and all had serious medical conditions they could not pay for because they had no insurance. We are trying to figure out how the plane tickets were paid for."

Bonnie sat back with that news. So a free trip to Vegas offering money or medical care really would make a great motivator for women to get on a plane.

Jacob went on. "Judy is running a search back through time with the women as best we can and finding the same pattern in general with all of them."

"Not a clue what that means," Cavanaugh said. "Other than someone is buying the tickets."

"Which helps explain how they could all be on the same day every year," Young said.

Bonnie just nodded. It was a pattern and that was more than they had so far.

"We also looked at family and relationships of the last five missing women," Jacob said. "Three of them, at one point or another over the year before they disappeared, had domestic issues with either a boyfriend or family member, bad enough to be reported. All five had no real family to speak of. When the women went missing, it was their jobs that reported them missing, not family, and the police in all five looked into possible murder by either family or boyfriend."

"Wow," Bonnie said. Another reason for those women to get on those planes.

"We'll see if that pattern holds going back as well," Jacob said. "As for Korat breed of cats, there are actually three members of a major cat association that say they have Korat cats in this area. Two sell kittens at times, but not official breeders, although both give papers with the kittens. And the kittens are not cheap, upwards of two thousand a cat."

"Any of them a sixty or seventy-year-old man?" Bonnie asked.

"No," Jacob said.

Bonnie sat back, stunned. She had been so hoping that this idea by Cavanaugh would link them to Woldstad.

"Who are they?" Cavanaugh asked.

"One is a twenty-year-old woman, student at UNLV," Jacob said. "She sells about six kittens a year."

"Nice money," Young said.

"The second is a single woman in her forties in Henderson

who does not sell kittens, and the third is a sixty-year-old married woman living on a ranch north of Las Vegas. She is married to a doctor and sells six or so kittens a year."

"Married to a doctor?" Bonnie asked, almost coming out of her chair over her phone.

"Yes," Jacob said. "And the student at UNLV is their daughter, majoring in pre-med."

"Could you send me their names and addresses," Bonnie asked.

"Already on the way to all of your phones," Jacob said. "I'll call you back when I have more."

With that he hung up and the sounds of the buffet around them came crashing back in as if Jacob's call had been a bubble holding everything away.

Bonnie looked at Cavanaugh, then at Young.

"You think maybe our suspect got married," Cavanaugh asked, "after he moved out of that house we were in this morning?"

"And kept killing?" Young asked.

Bonnie nodded. "Won't be the first time a serial killer has hidden in a family relationship."

"Looks like we are headed north," Young said, standing.

"I'll call Fawn," Cavanaugh said. "We need an active and back-up on this social call."

"Couldn't agree more," Bonnie said.

CHAPTER THIRTY-THREE

January 27th, 2019
Las Vegas, Nevada

Cavanaugh was driving, Bonnie beside him, Young in the back seat when Fawn called. They had just gotten past the point where the freeway dropped down into a four-lane road and soon would be only two lanes heading up through the desert toward Reno.

This time of the year, as they climbed out of the Las Vegas valley, the temperature just got colder by the mile. They had all brought their heavy coats just in case.

"On speaker with Bonnie and Young," Cavanaugh said.

"I'm waiting about a half-mile short of the ranch on the right side of the road," Fawn said.

"Three or four minutes behind you," Cavanaugh said.

"A couple things you should know," Fawn said. "This Dr. Francis is a long-time respected cancer researcher and also his farm up ahead is designated an official hospice."

Cavanaugh just shook his head at that.

"Think the guy's name was once Woldstad?" Young asked.

"It was," Fawn said. "But when he got married and moved out of that house we were in this morning, he officially changed his name to his wife's name and started to go by the name of Larry instead of Loch."

"No wonder there was no sign of him," Cavanaugh said.

"And we got the first body from the backyard out of the ground," Fawn said. "Third name on the list from Jacob. She was wrapped up tight in plastic, numbers of layers, actually, and she had her medical chart under her arms against her chest, just like the woman in the bed."

"Died of cancer?" Bonnie asked.

"That's what the chart says," Fawn said. "We won't know for sure until the bodies are examined completely at the morgue."

"Go to hell," Young said from the back seat.

Cavanaugh could not agree more as at that moment he pulled up behind Fawn. She was driving a deep blue Lexus that looked less than a year old. Clearly Fawn had some family money or was really good with her salary.

"Follow me in," she said, and hung up. A moment later she pulled back onto the highway going north.

"So this doctor was working on poor, abused women with cancer," Bonnie said.

"But that doesn't explain those two women with their face blown off in the cars," Young said, his voice sounding almost angry.

"That it does not," Cavanaugh said as he pulled back onto the highway to follow Detective Fawn up to a ranch that just might be the home of a very hidden and effective serial killer.

Or it might not.

They were soon going to find out one way or another.

The dirt driveway to the ranch was a good mile long, winding up toward some rocks and a ridgeline. Cavanaugh had to drop back a little behind Fawn's car because of the cloud of dust she was kicking up. Even in January this desert was dusty.

The ranch house was large, surrounded by tall oak and other types of shade trees that helped keep it cool in the summer. It looked very similar to the homes on his street, clearly built in the 1950s in a sprawling single-story ranch-house style. It was painted a dark brown with lighter brown trim that made the entire house blend into the rocks on the hill behind it.

The landscaping was rocks and flowers and very well done and clearly kept up. Cavanaugh could see three other buildings off to one side. One was larger and looked official with a sign over the door he couldn't read. The other two looked like guest cabins.

There were no other cars in the wide parking lot.

"Look at the cats," Bonnie said, pointing to one side where three cats lay on the top of a flat rock in the sun.

Now that she had pointed them out, he spotted at least five more cats of varied colors just as they drove in. None of them seemed concerned about the strange car in the slightest.

Fawn pulled up and stopped and Cavanaugh pulled in beside her, waiting for the dust to clear before opening his door.

The cold desert air hit him like a slap in the face and he almost went for his coat, then decided to just leave it. He doubted they would be out in the cold that long.

Bonnie and Young decided on the same thing.

Fawn got out last because, more than likely, she was calling in their location and getting some back-up close by. Cavanaugh hoped real close, in case things went real sour here.

"Let me do most of the talking," Fawn said. "And Young,

DEAN WESLEY SMITH

you hang back some, since you are not officially on the task force or on active."

He nodded to that.

Fawn turned toward the door. "So let's get this done before we all freeze what's left of our asses off."

"Old person joke?" Young asked.

"If the ass fits," Fawn said, "wear it."

Cavanaugh and Bonnie both laughed and with that they headed up the sidewalk.

As they reached the front door, it opened and they were greeted by an attractive and well-dressed woman about Bonnie and Fawn's age.

"Welcome," she said, smiling. "Can I help you?"

Cavanaugh wondered after she learned what they were there for if she would still be smiling.

He doubted it.

138

CHAPTER THIRTY-FOUR

January 27th, 2019
Las Vegas, Nevada

Bonnie stood to Fawn's right, and a step back, while Cavanaugh stood to Fawn's left and a few steps back. Both of them were watching the sides of the house and the windows. Bonnie liked the look of the home, but something felt off for some reason. Maybe because it might be a serial killer's home and they were not supposed to look comfortable.

"I'm Detective Fawn," Fawn said to the woman in the door. "These are Detectives Cavanaugh, State, and Young."

Fawn pointed to each of them in turn, then faced the woman.

"I'm Alice Francis. Wonderful to meet you all."

Fawn nodded. "We are here to talk with Loch Woldstad."

The woman's smile didn't alter. "That's my husband's original name, but now he goes by Dr. Larry Francis, my family name that he took when we got married. You could not believe how honored I felt when he did that."

She stepped back and said, "Come in out of the cold. I'll call him. He's in the clinic out back."

The blinds on the windows were open and the house felt warm and flooded with light. It looked very similar to Cavanaugh's home, with the charm of the older house kept in the walls and the style, yet the appliances and furniture had been updated to modern standards.

There were bookcases full of different types of books and the entire living room was warm and welcoming, with brown chairs and two large sofas. Very comfortable and homey, actually.

But again Bonnie felt that something was off.

Young stood to the side of the front door while Fawn moved deeper into the house behind the woman and Bonnie moved to the right and Cavanaugh to the left. None of them sat down.

"Hope you don't mind cats," the woman said.

She indicated two beautiful blue-gray cats sleeping together on a wide windowsill. They looked smallish, and Bonnie had a hunch they were Korats.

"You have any kittens at the moment?" Bonnie asked.

"Too early in the year," the woman said. "But we are hoping for some in April or May."

With that she clicked on what looked like an intercom on the wall near a large dining table. "Guests to see you."

"On my way," a voice said.

"So this is a hospice?" Fawn asked.

The woman nodded, some of her smile gone. "It is. We try to help poor and abused women from all over the country rest comfortably in the last days of their lives."

"Cancer?" Fawn asked.

The woman nodded. "Larry is an expert in the fight against cancer. His research is groundbreaking. The women who come here help him in his studies and he helps them as much as he can in return."

"Many drop into remission?" Fawn asked.

"A few, yes. But not enough by a long shot. Most are too far gone when they arrive here. We have far, far too many women buried up on the hill behind the clinic to ever suit my mind. But someday we will beat this disease."

Cavanaugh glanced at Bonnie at the mention of women buried up on the hill. His eyes were larger than normal. She had no idea if a permit was necessary to have a cemetery, but she was betting it was.

At that moment they heard the sound of the back door opening and closing and then a short elderly man, bald, and bent over slightly came in. He looked far, far older than his wife.

"Darling," the woman said, "these are detectives here to talk with you."

The doctor's face flinched, went slightly white, then he nodded.

Fawn introduced all three of them.

"We found your secret room in the house off Alta," Fawn said, diving right to the point.

Bonnie watched as Loch, or Larry, nodded, seemingly not surprised. More resigned.

"I had hoped to go back and move those poor women out here," he said, "but just never seemed to make it a priority when the house was between owners. There are so many of them there. Do you know most are out beyond the backyard fence line?"

Bonnie was shocked that this guy would just say that. Clearly he didn't think he did anything at all wrong.

"We found them and are in the process of removing them," Fawn said coldly.

"Their medical charts are buried with them," Larry said. "When you are done with your examination, is it possible to have them buried here with the others? And please don't notify their families. Their last wishes were to have no one know they had died and I have tried to honor those wishes."

Fawn glanced around at Young, who was looking like he was about to explode. She put her hand out to tell him to stay calm, then she turned back to Larry.

Bonnie didn't blame Young for being angry. After all the years and the memories of finding those first two women, he had a right.

"What about the first two you flew in?" Fawn asked Larry. "What happened to their bodies?"

With that Larry looked actually pained and he moved over and sat down at the head of the dining table.

Alice moved around behind him and put a hand on his shoulder, squeezing it slightly like he was a puppet and she was controlling.

"I lost them," Larry said, his voice low.

"Lost them?" Young asked, clear anger in his voice.

Fawn again indicated that Young should stay put and keep silent.

Larry didn't seem to notice. He just nodded. "I have no idea what happened to them."

"Would you care to explain that?" Fawn said.

"Let me get you a glass of water, dear," his wife said. She squeezed his shoulder again and kissed him on the forehead.

He thanked her and said he loved her and she said she loved him as she headed for the kitchen.

Weirdest damn exchange Bonnie had watched in a while.

Bonnie glanced at Cavanaugh, who was looking as puzzled as she felt.

Fawn just stared at the old guy who was not acting in any fashion like any serial killer Bonnie had every read about. But that didn't mean he wasn't.

But what this old guy looked like was someone who had almost lost the will to live suddenly. He seemed to be shrinking in on himself by the moment.

Something was going on. Bonnie could feel it, but she had no idea what.

All four of them stood, waiting in silence. The two cats just slept in the sun on the windowsill.

Larry sat at the big dining room table, bent over slightly, his hands on his lap, seemingly lost in his own thoughts, waiting for his glass of water.

At that moment Bonnie's phone beeped with a text. And so did Cavanaugh's and Young's and Fawn's.

Text was from Jacob.

Text said simply, *"Caution! Wife might be the killer! Caution!"*

PART FIVE

The Showdown

CHAPTER THIRTY-FIVE

January 27th, 2019
Las Vegas, Nevada

Cavanaugh stared at the text from Jacob for a moment, not really believing what he was seeing.

Cavanaugh quickly returned a text, typing on his phone faster than he had believed he could.

"Young! Gun in glove box."

Fawn nodded to Young as he looked up from Cavanaugh's text.

"Excuse me," Young said into the silence. "I need to step outside for a moment."

The old doctor sitting at the table said nothing and didn't seem to notice.

Cavanaugh was glad that Young was going for a gun. He had no idea what kind of information Jacob had found, but he somehow knew where they were and felt the need to warn them. And Cavanaugh trusted Jacob completely.

Young clicked the front door closed behind him and that seemed to get the doctor to notice.

He reached under the table and before Cavanaugh could realize what had happened, the doctor had a gun out from where it must have been hidden under the table and pointed it up under his chin.

The man's finger was on the trigger and he was holding the gun with both hands.

Cavanaugh had his gun out almost as quickly, as did Bonnie and Fawn. All three had their guns leveled on the doctor.

Fawn moved sideways and looked into the kitchen, then shook her head, meaning that she couldn't see Alice anywhere. The woman had left her husband and was trying to run.

"Doctor, what are you doing?" Fawn asked, her voice amazingly soft and in control.

"What I should have done years ago," he said softly. "But she kept me believing that my research was worth those women's lives, that in the end I would be honored as a hero for saving lives. And over the years, you know, I actually started to believe her."

"So what did you do?" Fawn asked. "What did she do?"

"We both loved cats," the doctor said. "Alice started out as a young patient of mine, not cancer, just an injury from when her mother hit her. Alice offered to help me with the pack of cats I was feeding. And she wanted to breed Korats because she had read about them in some book, so I bought a breeding champion pair and she came to my house and took care of them for me."

Cavanaugh stood completely silent, making sure he didn't break the flow of what the doctor was saying.

"How old was she at that point?" Fawn asked.

"A very mature fourteen," the doctor said. "And she was

interested in me and my work and I was flattered. I had never had time for anyone else with medical school, so attention by anyone was like a drug."

He smiled fondly at what must have been a memory.

Cavanaugh glanced at Bonnie who was just slowly shaking her head. As detectives, they had heard a lot of things over the years, but some things just never stopped disgusting Cavanaugh.

"What about her family?" Fawn asked.

"She had no real family. A drunk mother, no one else even noticed she was spending time at my home. We both so loved cats."

The entire time the doctor talked, the gun never wavered from under his chin and Cavanaugh had zero doubt he would use it. Clearly the doctor felt comfortable with what he was about to do. Must have thought about it a lot.

And to have it planted under the kitchen table like that must have meant that he and Alice had expected a visit from the police at some point.

"Alice wanted me to bring in women who needed help that were suffering from different forms of cancer so I could study them," the doctor went on without Fawn prompting him.

"Alice contacted them, arranged to have them come in, and I sent the money to pay for their travel. She always picked women from homes and lives that the women did not want to return to."

He stopped talking and after a moment Fawn asked, "And then what happened?"

Cavanaugh noticed that both Fawn and Bonnie had their phones out and next to them and were recording. Both their guns still pointed at the doctor. Smart thinking on both of their parts.

"After about six months," the doctor said, "I thought I was

making a little progress with my first patient when she suddenly died. I was devastated and Alice said she would take care of the body, get it to the right place, and arrange for another woman to take her spot."

"How did she do that?" Fawn asked, her voice remaining low and in control, something Cavanaugh was very impressed with.

"That was the point we first slept together," the doctor said. "I know we shouldn't have, but I was madly in love and listening to her. That was when she took control of me completely."

Cavanaugh was getting more and more disgusted at what he was hearing. Bonnie was still just shaking her head.

"So Alice had me rent her a car with false ID that she had gotten somewhere and I helped her load the body into the car. I never asked what she did with those first two bodies."

"So what was happening with the women?" Fawn asked. "Why were they dying?"

The doctor took a deep breath. "The first years they all would have died anyway from their cancers, but Alice saved the women the pain and suffering and put them to sleep, as you would a cat who was suffering."

Cavanaugh wanted to be sick.

"I did not know for years what was happening," the doctor said, "and when I learned, she convinced me it was better for the women to die peacefully in their sleep then be taken in the last stages of cancer. I should have gone to the police then, but I did not. I was completely under her control. Still am. It will be a relief to finally be free."

He took a deep breath and then said simply, "I always thought she would euthanize me in my sleep one day. Seems she has left it up to me, now, to be done with all this."

"You know you don't have to do this," Fawn said, her voice soft and level as it had been all along.

"I started off a doctor to save lives," he said, his voice stronger. "If you had let as many women be killed as I have by a monster your found yourself married to, you would have to do this as well. No, you would want to do this."

He shook his head, then said, "I just hope some of my research survives me. I think it's good work and might actually be of help to others someday."

The sound of the shot was amazingly loud in the closed space.

CHAPTER THIRTY-SIX

January 27th, 2019
Las Vegas, Nevada

Bonnie's ears were ringing from the shot that seemed in slow motion to take the top off the doctor's head and smear it all over the wall and the window where the two cats were sleeping.

Both of the cats, tracking blood as they went, flashed into the kitchen and vanished.

"Son of a bitch," Fawn said, holstering her gun, then grabbing her phone and turning off the recording before tucking it back into her pocket.

Bonnie did the same thing. They both had all that recorded. And it was damned lucky none of them had been behind the doctor and in the blood and brains spray. Now the doctor's body was just sitting in the chair, what was left of his head back. His arms were at his side and the gun had ended up a few feet away.

Typical suicide scene that she had seen more times than she

wanted to see. But this was the first time that she had witnessed one. She could have gone the rest of her life without that.

"We got to find Alice!" Cavanaugh said as he turned for the front door. "His speech and confession gave her a pretty good head start."

Bonnie glanced around. There was no way through the blood and brain parts to get to the kitchen, so they were going to need to go out and around.

Bonnie went through the front door right behind Cavanaugh and Fawn followed.

The biting cold winter air cleared her mind and pushed back a little that scene inside. Thank heavens the sun was shining. That helped a lot as well.

Young was beside the car, a gun in his hand, looking worried.

"Doc killed himself," Cavanaugh said. "Alice has been euthanizing the women like animals."

"And she was the one who took care of the first two women in the cars," Bonnie said to Young. "Doc confessed it all to buy Alice time to escape."

Then she and Fawn, guns drawn again, headed around the right side of the house while Cavanaugh and Young went around the other side.

"This escape was all planned," Fawn said, reaching the side of the house and peaking around the corner. "More than likely Alice is away from the house somewhere. But I doubt she would be stupid enough to be in one of the outbuildings."

"I'm betting on a tunnel out of the house," Bonnie said, "leading away from the house. Somewhere there is a car and a back road out of here."

"Shit," Fawn said, holstering her gun and taking out her

phone to call in a helicopter and more forces and medical and morgue.

Bonnie stepped away from the house and studied the back hillside covered in rocks and brush. Most of the year that area would be full of snakes and who knew what else, but in this cold, it would be fairly safe to go up that way.

At that moment Cavanaugh and Young came around the other side of the house, moving slowly and staying in cover, both their guns drawn.

Cavanaugh shook his head as they headed toward Bonnie and Fawn, ducking under windows as they came.

"Betting a secret way out of the house," Bonnie said to Cavanaugh in a whisper loud enough for him to hear through the cold, crisp air.

"Agree," Cavanaugh said. "Young, I think you should stay with Fawn until help arrives. Bonnie and I will head up into the rocks to see what we can see."

Fawn turned and clicked off her phone. "Back-up headed up the driveway, helicopter a good ten to twelve minutes out."

Bonnie looked up into the rocks. "The doctor gave her so much time, I'm afraid if we don't get eyes on her up there, we might lose her in ten minutes."

"Go," Fawn said to Cavanaugh and Bonnie. "Young, take up a spot on that back corner of the house in cover, I'll take the front corner. If she's still in there, we got to keep her in there."

Bonnie nodded and guns once again drawn, she and Cavanaugh headed across the open yard at a run toward the rocks and a trail that led upward. By the time she reached the rocks, she remembered why being a cop was a young person's job.

CHAPTER THIRTY-SEVEN

January 27th, 2019
Las Vegas, Nevada

Cavanaugh felt like it was taking them forever to climb up the dirt path through the rocks. He had no idea where it was going, but he had a hunch Alice was a ways ahead of them. She must have had another way out of the house besides the back door that they would have heard.

The cold air made it easier and the sun actually felt good. But his hands were just about as cold as he could remember them being.

Bonnie was following and staying with him. More than likely he was the one slowing her down. He definitely needed to spend more time at the gym if being on this Cold Poker Gang task force required this kind of exercise.

"This path sure seems well-maintained," Bonnie said, clearly as out of breath as he was.

"Well-used," Cavanaugh said.

About two hundred feet up the hill, they stopped and looked back. The house and the outbuildings were clear and the sidewalk between each building was trimmed in plants and winter flowers. He could see Young and Fawn both tucked against the corners of the main house.

"I wonder how many women are in those other buildings?" Bonnie said.

"Got a hunch we're about to find out," Cavanaugh said, pointing to the clouds of dust being kicked up by cars streaming up the driveway.

He turned and kept climbing, wondering why such a well-worn and maintained path was here. His question was answered as they crested a shallow ridge and found a large area of green grass covered by crosses filling a shallow valley.

More crosses than Cavanaugh wanted to count.

"Graveyard," Bonnie said, her voice soft and clearly out of breath.

The graveyard sat in a small valley and had a large wooden garage-like building to one side

At that point the sound of a car engine started up inside the garage and a garage door slid upward.

At a run, Cavanaugh started across the graveyard and the green grass toward the garage.

A white Lincoln SUV pulled out and turned away from the graveyard and the house.

Alice was driving. She waved and smiled at them like she was pulling out of her garage in a normal neighborhood.

She turned and gunned the SUV away from them, heading between two large rocks and vanishing over a crest of a hill.

"Damn it all to hell," Bonnie said, clearly winded. She grabbed her phone and got Fawn.

"Alice is in a white SUV headed away from the house. Green

cemetery in the rocks at the top of the hill behind the house is where she started."

Cavanaugh holstered his gun and started toward the rocks beyond the cemetery.

"Damn," Bonnie said, clicking off her phone and following Cavanaugh. "The helicopter is still a good five to ten minutes out."

"Not sure where Alice thinks she's going to go in this desert," Cavanaugh said, "that we can't find her, but let's see where that road heads just in case."

"Good idea."

It took them almost no time at all to climb up to the ridge behind the cemetery. At the top Cavanaugh was stunned at the drop on the other side. It was steep, very steep. Almost cliff-like down into a hidden and wide green valley on the other side.

"There she is," Bonnie said, pointing to the right as the sound of the car engine echoed among the rocks.

The road went to the right after leaving the cemetery, then from what Cavanaugh could tell, it switched back and went directly under them across the face of the steep mountain, then switched back again, making its way under them along the steep, rock-covered hill.

Down in that valley at the bottom were lots of trees and ranches stretching into the distance and places she could hide from a helicopter search. And she would be in that valley in just minutes.

"How good is your throwing arm?" Cavanaugh asked.

"Used to be pretty good."

Cavanaugh quickly looked around to find a couple of soft-ball-sized rocks. From this height of a good ten stories above where Alice was going to go under them, a rock that size might do some real damage. Or at least slow her down some.

Bonnie pointed to a large boulder that seemed to be just sitting on the edge of the slope. "Let's shove that over first, see if it can block that road."

"Great idea."

He and Bonnie worked for a moment, rocking the chair-sized boulder, until it went over the edge, tumbling down the slope and kicking up other rocks and boulders as it went in a miniature rockslide.

Alice in her white SUV had made the first switchback and was speeding back toward where the rocks were headed.

The big boulder hit the road ahead of her and went right on over in a cloud of dust, heading for the road below.

Cavanaugh stood there with a rock in his hand and watched as a few medium-sized rocks the boulder had dislodged stopped on the road and dust swirled in the air. Alice was going to have to stop and push those aside to get by.

But Alice didn't slow down in the slightest. She hit a rock about the size of a small dog and the SUV bounced.

Hard.

With a nasty grating sound that made Cavanaugh wince.

The SUV bounced again as the rock smashed into the underside and the front tire hit another smaller rock.

The next thing that happened was in slow motion as the SUV went over the edge and started to tumble just as the rocks had.

End over end over end.

The sound of the crash filled the air like thunder as more and more rocks joined the tumble and the car hit the road below and bounced even higher.

Alice was ejected from the car like a rag doll being tossed away by an angry kid. She spun violently through the air and smashed into some large rocks as the SUV continued to tumble down the hill, finally stopping in a cloud of dust.

The sound of rocks continuing to hit the SUV rang through the air for a few moments.

Then the desert went back to its normal silence.

"She really should have stopped," Bonnie said after a moment of both of them standing there in shock at what had happened below them. "Think she's still alive?"

"I hope so," Cavanaugh said. "Because I really want her to suffer for what she did to all those women."

"I couldn't agree more," Bonnie said.

But Cavanaugh noticed that neither one of them made a move to start down the hill toward Alice. She just wasn't worth the climb.

CHAPTER THIRTY-EIGHT

February 7th, 2019
Las Vegas, Nevada

Bonnie couldn't believe how much had happened since the last time they walked out of a Cold Poker Gang meeting and she saw the momma cat. Two weeks of movement. And now in her hand she had her and Cavanaugh's third case.

Neither of them had even looked at it yet.

The night was a warm one for early February. Comfortable to be out without a coat, actually. No wind, clear skies, just perfect.

And both she and Cavanaugh were feeling great.

Andor hadn't given them a new case last week because they were still working with Detective Fawn and Jacob to clean up all the details about all the women killed by Larry and Alice Francis. Turned out there were not just the nineteen bodies at the house and the two originally left in cars, but over ninety in the cemetery on the hill.

And each one was going to have to be tested to see if the woman died of cancer or was killed.

What had caused Jacob to call and warn them when they were in the house was the preliminary autopsy on the body in the basement had not only shown stage four cancer, but extremely high doses of pentobarbital, a drug commonly used to euthanize animals.

Jacob had done a quick search and discovered that Alice had ordered quantities of the drug for years for her cat care, far more than a small breeder would need or ever use. That's why he had traced Bonnie and Cavanaugh's cell phone locations, knew they were all in the house, and had warned them by text.

From what Fawn and Jacob had put together, Dr. Larry Francis was a respected researcher on stage four levels of cancer, and had become immensely wealthy in his work. But Alice ran everything. All his money, finding the women, everything.

In fact, numbers of doctors in the cancer field had said they hadn't seen him at all in over a decade. Alice had kept him locked on their ranch.

And Alice had died in the car wreck, appropriately enough considering how the case started, with her face smashed beyond recognition against a rock.

Turns out their daughter did not know what her mother was doing, and she ended up taking all the cats.

"So, what's the plan?" Cavanaugh asked as they reached his car and got in. "Dinner and look over the new case?"

Bonnie looked around at the quiet neighborhood, then tossed the case file on the back seat. "How about just dinner. We can look at the case tomorrow."

"Perfect," Cavanaugh said.

"I'm thinking a juicy burger and fries and a milkshake," Bonnie said.

Cavanaugh laughed and started the car. "I just might know a place."

"It better be good," Bonnie said, laughing with him.

"The best in town," Cavanaugh said.

Bonnie just sat back and enjoyed the drive toward the downtown area. And enjoyed the company of her partner. Someone she now couldn't imagine not knowing.

CHAPTER THIRTY-NINE

February 7th, 2019
Las Vegas, Nevada

Cavanaugh really enjoyed the hamburger and fries, and the milkshake Madge made for them to share was beyond imagination. And now they were back at his place.

And her place as well.

As they got out of the car in his driveway, they both just stopped and enjoyed the warm evening and the fresh air and the sky full of stars. Even though the house was close to the downtown area, the trees around them blocked most of the light and the stars really seemed to come out at times.

"What a beautiful night," Bonnie said after a moment.

"After the last two weeks," Cavanaugh said, "this is exactly what is needed. I almost said, 'the doctor ordered' but changed my mind."

Bonnie laughed.

Since they had finished the last case, not only had they been helping Fawn and Jacob clean up the massive amount of details with Dr. Larry Francis and his deadly wife, Alice, but they had moved most of Bonnie's things into the apartment.

It felt fantastic to have her so close, as if his house wasn't just sleeping anymore. His house, for the first time, felt alive and a place he wanted to spend time in.

And that felt different and very wonderful.

Of course, the family of cats helped as well. Little Momma, as they called her, had turned out to be a real love and pretty much demanded to be petted at all times of the day or night. And Cavanaugh didn't mind in the slightest.

And Little Momma's two kittens were growing like crazy. Bonnie had suggested after a conversation with the vet that they put down some layers of blankets in Bonnie's laundry room and move the top of the cat carrier in there near the cat box so Little Momma could train the kittens to use it when the time came.

And the little ones were now old enough to try some soft food. Not much, but just a little.

And the two kittens still had no names, although the topic was a regular one between them. Cavanaugh was leaning toward Player for the orange one and Leap for the black and white. Bonnie wanted to call them movie names like Luke and Leia.

No decision had been made and Cavanaugh figured the kittens would just name themselves eventually by their traits.

So, when they got home from dinner, Bonnie led the way into her apartment to see how the family was doing and give Little Momma some fresh soft food.

Bonnie had made the apartment even cozier than it already was, with pictures on the walls, a runner and flowers on the dining room table, and coffee maker in the kitchen. They had switched out the old fridge for a brand new state-of-the-art one, but otherwise left things alone.

She had also brought in a television for her living room and another for her bedroom.

"You up for a movie?" Cavanaugh asked.

"Sounds wonderful," Bonnie said. "Let me change clothes and I'll be right in.

"I'll make the popcorn," Cavanaugh said, turning to go back into his part of the house.

"Oh, I am so full," Bonnie said.

Cavanaugh didn't even glance back. "There is always room for popcorn."

"Torturer," Bonnie said, laughing.

Fifteen minutes later they were side-by-side on the couch in his television room and he was cuing *Jumanji* up, a comedy they had both said they wanted to see.

He had a massive tub of popcorn on the coffee table in front of them and two bowls. He had changed into his favorite Golden Knights sweatshirt and jogging pants and slippers and when Bonnie came in from her apartment, she had on a large sweatshirt with a cat on it and shorts and slippers.

She turned down the lights before she came to sit on the couch beside him and put her feet up.

"Damn, I needed a night like this," she said.

"So did I," Cavanaugh said. "Perfect, just perfect."

At that moment Little Momma came in from Bonnie's apartment, announced her presence and jumped up on the couch between them.

After some pets, she curled up between them, facing the television screen, purring, clearly waiting for the movie to start.

"I was wrong," Cavanaugh said.

"About what?" Bonnie asked.

"A minute ago I said this was perfect. But now, with a cat between us, it really is."

Bonnie laughed and petted Little Momma as Cavanaugh started the movie and the previous few weeks were forgotten and only a really fun movie lay ahead.

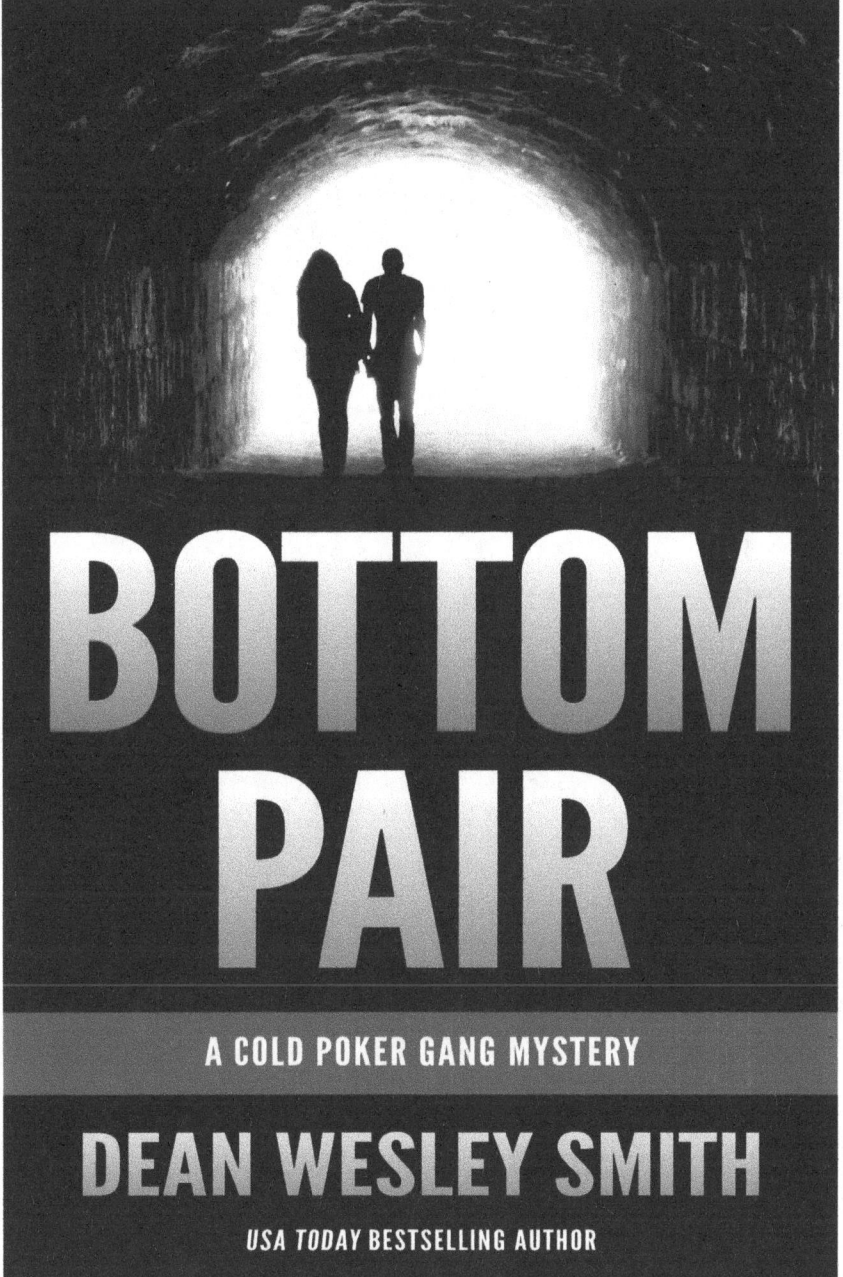

BOTTOM PAIR

A COLD POKER GANG MYSTERY

DEAN WESLEY SMITH

USA TODAY BESTSELLING AUTHOR

The Cold Poker Gang Mysteries continue with the next book in the series, Bottom
Pair. *Following is a sample chapter from that book*

PROLOGUE

March 18th, 2002
Henderson, Nevada

Sandy Goodson loved the early mornings in Henderson. Especially in the spring when it hadn't gotten too hot yet. From the front door of her three-bedroom home in the Deep Canyon Heights subdivision, she could see the casinos of the Strip in Las Vegas stretching away from her.

The sun, just peaking over the hills to the east, lit the casinos up like beacons in the early morning light.

She loved the home that she had just bought last year, even though at the moment it felt too big for her. She loved the Strip, and she loved working there. She couldn't believe how lucky she had gotten to get a job in hospitality at the Luxor Hotel. A dream job that paid her a lot for doing what she loved, helping people and talking with them. And it gave her a chance to meet people; people who have ended up important in her life.

She stood on her front porch enjoying the coolness of the

morning air for a minute, going through her normal checklist, making sure she was ready. She stood five-five, had long blonde hair that while working she kept pulled back and away from her face.

Susan, her best friend in the entire world, said she looked wonderful with her hair pulled back or down around her face. Sandy trusted Susan and just thinking of her made Sandy smile.

Sandy checked her purple uniform, a color that didn't go well with her pale skin, but other employees she worked with said just wait and that will change. The Luxor always switched out their uniforms every six months or so. She didn't worry about it at this point.

She had on sneakers that she would change out for high heels as soon as she got to the employee locker room, and she checked to make sure her dress shoes were in her bag. They were.

And her Luxor ID was in her bag along with her purse.

Everything exactly as she always did every morning. Nothing at all different. She had made sure of that.

She was ready, keys in her hand, so she pulled closed and locked her front door, not letting herself look back.

With one last look at the Strip in the distance, she climbed into her white 2001 Subaru that she called Horse that she had bought for herself when she got the job at the Luxor.

She pulled out of her driveway, the streets of the subdivision deserted in the early morning hours. She went past the security cameras at the front gate at almost exactly the same time she did every morning and turned right toward the Strip.

She was smiling, anticipating and yet worried about the day ahead of her.

That was the last anyone ever saw of her.

She vanished without a trace, and six months later her

missing person's case went cold and she was pretty much forgotten.

Two years later her younger sister, Reese, sold Sandy's car, which was found parked on a side street just off the Strip. Because of the mortgage payments, Reese also sold Sandy's wonderful house.

But Reese never stopped looking for Sandy. It seemed that for almost twenty years, Reese was the only one.

NEWSLETTER SIGN-UP

Be the first to know!

Just sign up for the Dean Wesley Smith newsletter, and keep up with the latest news, releases and so much more—even the occasional giveaway.

So, what are you waiting for? To sign up go to deanwesleysmith.com.

But wait! There's more. Sign up for the WMG Publishing newsletter, too, and get the latest news and releases from all of the WMG authors and lines, including Kristine Kathryn Rusch, Kristine Grayson, Kris Nelscott, *Smith's Monthly, Pulphouse Fiction Magazine* and so much more.

To sign up go to wmgpublishing.com.

ABOUT THE AUTHOR

Considered one of the most prolific writers working in modern fiction, *USA Today* bestselling writer Dean Wesley Smith published almost two hundred novels in forty years, and hundreds and hundreds of short stories across many genres.

At the moment he produces novels in several major series, including the time travel Thunder Mountain novels set in the Old West, the galaxy-spanning Seeders Universe series, the urban fantasy Ghost of a Chance series, a superhero series starring Poker Boy, and a mystery series featuring the retired detectives of the Cold Poker Gang.

His monthly magazine, *Smith's Monthly*, which consists of only his own fiction, premiered in October 2013 and offers readers more than 70,000 words per issue, including a new and original novel every month.

During his career, Dean also wrote a couple dozen *Star Trek* novels, the only two original *Men in Black* novels, Spider-Man and X-Men novels, plus novels set in gaming and television worlds. Writing with his wife Kristine Kathryn Rusch under the name Kathryn Wesley, he wrote the novel for the NBC miniseries The Tenth Kingdom and other books for *Hallmark Hall of Fame* movies.

He wrote novels under dozens of pen names in the worlds of comic books and movies, including novelizations of almost a dozen films, from *The Final Fantasy* to *Steel* to *Rundown*.

Dean also worked as a fiction editor off and on, starting at Pulphouse Publishing, then at *VB Tech Journal*, then Pocket Books, and now at WMG Publishing, where he and Kristine Kathryn Rusch serve as series editors for the acclaimed *Fiction River* anthology series, which launched in 2013. In 2018, WMG Publishing Inc. launched the first issue of the reincarnated *Pulphouse Fiction Magazine*, with Dean reprising his role as editor.

For more information about Dean's books and ongoing projects, please visit his website at www.deanwesleysmith.com and sign up for his newsletter.

www.ingramcontent.com/pod-product-compliance
Lightning Source LLC
Chambersburg PA
CBHW011137100726
47898CB00009B/3013